The T-Zone

Bill Hansmann

Copyright 2019 Bill Hansmann

This is a work of fiction. The names, events, and characters are fictitious and any resemblance to actual persons living or dead or locales is coincidental except those instances named in author's notes and acknowledgments.

ISBN: 9781798649152

Also by Bill Hansmann

Once Bitten

To Abner Doubleday

Prologue

It was opening night of the 2019 baseball season. The crowd of just over forty-one thousand at Sun Trust Park, home of the Atlanta Braves, excitedly awaited the first pitch. Last season had shown great improvement in the team's rebuilding efforts, as they had won their division race and made it to the postseason for the first time in five years.

This year promised even greater results, with a possible trip to the World Series awaiting. Of course, every team was undefeated on the first day of the season, but Braves fans were highly optimistic that the present club would reward their patience with even greater glory than did their teams of the '90s and early 2000s.

The stadium was decked out as stadiums always are for opening day. The grass was incredibly green, helped out in a few stubborn spots by the grounds crew's application of paint that matched the color of the grass perfectly.

Red, white and blue bunting hung from the second deck surrounding the outfield. The white chalk marking the border between fair and foul territory and creating the batter's boxes was pristine, and perfectly applied. The dirt of the infield was expertly raked, and the periphery of the playing field manicured meticulously. The fans were ready for the season to get under way.

The opponents for the first game of the new season were the Miami Marlins. Marlin fans were not as optimistic; every year, it seemed, they found a new way to lose. What the Marlins did have was Miguel Fernandez, the star who had defected from Cuba almost six years ago and had been the subject of a frenzied bidding war for his baseball talents. Miami had won that battle and the Marlin organization had been well rewarded.

Fernandez had been an immediate sensation and was now, entering his fifth major league season, the reigning National League batting champion and Most Valuable Player. The switch-hitting star stepped into the right-handed batter's box and prepared for the first pitch from the Braves' lefty. The season was about to begin.

***

The *T-Zone* is an area of the human head that includes the forehead, nose and chin. It is known to all snipers as the area to hit if you are aiming for a headshot kill. In fact, most snipers would tell you to forget about the chin and lower third of the nose: you need to hit the forehead, between the eyes or at the top of the nose. The smarter kill shot, of course, is always center mass of the body, since head shots outside the T-Zone do not always kill; but they *are* messy and dramatic.

Three hundred fifty yards away, hidden on the roof of the new Omni Hotel overlooking the stadium, a figure in black waited patiently. Authorities later would say that it should have been impossible for anyone to be in that location. Yet the dark-clad figure *was* there—with his .300 Win Mag sniper rifle outfitted with an Accuracy International AICS 2.0 folding stock, an MIRS Rail System and a Nightforce NXS 8-32x56 scope mounted on a Harris 89-inch Swivel Bipod.

When a sniper rifle is fired, the controlled explosion inside the weapon produces fifty thousand pounds per square inch of pressure, forcing the full metal jacketed hollow point projectile down the barrel and out the end of the weapon at thirty-four hundred feet per second, more than three times the speed of sound. The accuracy of the shot is wholly dependent on the skill of the shooter. The man on the roof of the Omni Hotel was highly skilled.

As Fernandez waited for the first pitch, the 7.62 NATO round hit him just above the nose and between the eyes, the center of the T-Zone. He was dead before anyone in the stadium even knew there had been a shot. His blood and brain matter were sprayed over the Braves' catcher and the home plate umpire, a scene captured by live TV and dozens of sports photographers present for the event. The baseball season was under way.

1

Linda Atkinson was hanging up the phone as her husband, Mike, entered the office. Mike and Linda, along with Linda's brother, Tommy Cevilli, made up the Atkinson Detective Agency in Marietta, Georgia.

The agency was originally just Mike and Linda. Mike was a former Atlanta Police Department detective and Linda, a former professor of criminology at Georgia State University in downtown Atlanta. Tommy only recently had come aboard full time, after years of employment as an IT technician.

"I can't believe I'm saying this, Mike," said Linda, "but I wish the phone would *stop* ringing. At least for a little while."

The agency, located less than a mile from the Big Chicken, a beloved Marietta landmark, had been struggling until just under a year ago. Then Mike, Linda and Tommy had solved the murder of Michelle Simons and succeeded in getting the man convicted of her killing, Keith Michaels, freed from death row.

Michelle's true murderer was her husband, Dr. Jerry Simons, who had orchestrated an almost perfect frame job of Michaels.

Michaels' sister hired the agency to prove her brother was not the killer, and they were successful. Simons had died on the Atkinson home's kitchen floor, bleeding out from a severed carotid artery, but not before having confessed to his wife's murder and two others as well.

That confession, recorded on Tommy's cell phone, was the piece of evidence that exonerated Michaels and allowed him to be freed. The Atkinsons' son, Mikey, had played a major, though unintentional, part when he interrupted the scene between Simons and his parents. Simons, fully expecting to shoot both Mike and Linda, was bragging about his murders. Mikey's entrance distracted the killer, who fired wildly at Mikey and missed—allowing Mike to incapacitate the wife-murdering doctor by spearing him with the shaft of a broken golf club. The throat wound caused Simons to bleed out in seconds.

"We may have to hire more people," said Mike. The part-time receptionist new to their staff was unable to work all the hours needed. "We may have to let Susie go and get someone full time to answer the phone. I hate to do it, but I know you sure as hell don't want to spend half your life on the phone."

Since solving the Simons murder, their little agency had become the hottest P.I. firm in the whole metro area, if not the entire southeast of the country. There had been a tremendous amount of publicity, never a bad thing for a struggling business, as long as it was good. This publicity had been *very* good. The three were depicted as brilliant detectives who solved a crime that the police and courts had gotten wrong.

"Let's see if we can keep Susie *and* hire another secretary full time," said Linda. "We're so busy that I'm sure we can find plenty for two people to do. Besides, Susie is using her income to pay her way through college. She's majoring in criminology and you know that's a subject near and dear to me."

"Hey, guys," Tommy entered, interrupting. "Are we finally finished with the Miller case?"

"I gave everything we have to the Cobb County sheriff," said Mike. "I think they should be able to handle it from here. I can't believe they couldn't stop that sick bastard without our help." The sick bastard here referred to a local high school gym teacher accused of sexual impropriety involving several of his students.

Their conversation again was interrupted, this time by the phone.

"Atkinson Detective Agency," Linda answered. "How can I help you?"

She listened for almost a minute. "Okay, give me your contact information and I'll get back to you within the hour." Hanging up, she turned to Mike and Tommy. "You guys aren't going to believe this. That was a friend of Mark Alan's, who wants us to help prove he was not the SunTrust Park shooter."

"You've got to be shitting me!" exclaimed Tommy. "They arrested Alan coming out of the hotel with the rifle in his hand. I was at the game that night with my dad. I'll never forget what happened."

The killing of Miguel Fernandez in front of forty-one thousand stadium spectators and hundreds of thousands more watching it live on tv was the most spectacular televised event since the hijacked plane hit the World Congress Center's south tower.

Former U.S. Marine sniper Mark Alan had been apprehended just outside the Omni Hotel less than forty-five minutes after the shooting. His protestations of innocence fell on deaf ears. The weapon in his possession at the time he was taken into custody was proven by ballistic testing to be the murder

12

weapon. Alan was currently in the Cobb County Jail, awaiting trial. His conviction appeared to be a foregone conclusion.

"This feels a little bit too familiar," said Mike. "You're sure it wasn't his sister calling?"—a joking reference to Diane Morgan, sister of Keith Michaels, the man they proved innocent in the Michelle Simons killing.

"No," said Linda. "The caller says he served with Alan in Iraq and he's positive Alan was framed. This really does sound familiar. At least Alan's not on death row. He hasn't even gone to trial yet."

"I suppose it's worth talking to the guy. Remember, we were convinced that trying to get Michaels off was a waste of time. Maybe lightning does strike twice," said Mike.

"But walking out with the murder weapon and him being a trained sniper? We're supposed to get him off? I don't think even David Copperfield would attempt that trick," said Tommy, "although I did hear Copperfield once made the Statue of Liberty disappear, so stranger things have happened. I guess we should at least hear him out."

"So, we agree," said Linda. "we'll see what this guy has to say?"

Tommy and Mike both voiced yes.

"We've done everything we can on the Miller case and the cops have it," said Tommy. "We have lots of stuff going on, but nothing as big as this would be if it turns out to be worth pursuing."

"Okay then," said Linda. "I'll call him back. His name is Greg Palkot. I'll set it up as soon as possible."

***

The next morning, the three were at the agency office when a man entered the reception area.

"I'm Greg Palkot." They shook hands all around. "I'm here to tell you that there's no way Mark Alan is the SunTrust Park shooter."

Palkot had a military bearing, his rigid posture and formal manner that of one who took seriously the warrior lifestyle. Only the shaggy cut of his light brown hair suggested that he was no longer active duty.

A shade over six feet tall, he was approximately one hundred eighty lean pounds, with brilliant, sapphire-blue eyes that glowed with an angry intensity. Mike and Tommy both thought at once they would never want to go up against this guy in a fight.

14

"Alan was captured less than an hour after the shooting, leaving the scene of the crime and carrying the murder weapon," said Mike. "Plus, he was a marine sniper. Fernandez was killed by a sniper. It's pretty hard to imagine that he wasn't the killer."

"I know as well as anyone how bad it looks and how guilty he appears," said Palkot. "But I'll stake my life on the fact that he didn't do it."

"How can you be so sure he wasn't the shooter?" asked Linda.

"Because I'm the one who handed him the case with the rifle in it to carry out the door of the Omni Hotel."

"What the fuck?" Tommy blurted out. "Are you saying that *you* were the shooter?"

"No. I wasn't," said Palkot.

"Well then, what the fuck *are* you saying?" Mike demanded.

"Let me add my *what the fuck?* as well," offered Linda.

"It's a long story," Palkot began. "Parts of it are going to seem unlikely, or even impossible to you. But I swear on my daughter's eyes it's the truth."

15

"Well, you certainly have our attention," said Mike. "We're all ears."

2

"I have a five-year-old daughter named Leah. Her mother and I are divorced. Leah and Molly, her mom, were living in Columbus, Georgia, just outside of Fort Benning. Three days before the shooting, my daughter was kidnapped."

"Kidnapped?" asked Mike. "Is she okay?"

"Yes, she's fine and back with her mother. They've gone to Colorado to stay with Molly's parents."

"That's certainly good to hear. Did you call the police when it happened?"

"No, I didn't," said Palkot. "I got a call at about four thirty in the morning. Whoever was on the other end of the line was using a voice distorter, so I couldn't even tell if it was a man or a woman, it just sounded like Darth Vader. But the voice said they had my daughter and that if I called the police, I'd never see her again. I was told to make sure my ex-wife didn't call the police either, and that I would hear from them the next day."

"What did you do? You must have been frantic," said Linda.

"I immediately called Molly. She didn't even know Leah was gone. She accused me of playing some cruel prank by calling her in the early hours of the morning. When she went to Leah's room and saw that our daughter really *was* gone, she went nuts."

"Then what?" asked Tommy.

"I drove down from Atlanta, where I was living, as fast as I could. I had to get there quickly to calm Molly down, even though I was going crazy myself. I had convinced her not to call the police before I arrived. It took me almost two hours to get to Columbus, and when I did arrive, Molly was nearly berserk. She had failed to set the home alarm system the night before, and the kidnapper came right in through Leah's bedroom window.

"I was torn about whether or not to call the police, and I had to convince Molly to hear me out. The authorities always say that you should make the call, that it's the best hope to get your child back, but I wasn't so sure."

"Why not?" asked Linda.

"I'm only thirty-nine years old, but I'm a big Frank Sinatra fan. I was always fascinated by the story about his son,

18

Frank Junior's, kidnapping. The story became a sensation after the fact, but Sinatra managed to keep the media and the local police out of it while it was going on, and he was able to negotiate a ransom and get his son back.

"He *personally* negotiated with the kidnappers. He turned down offers of assistance from Bobby Kennedy's Justice Department and from mob boss Sam Giancana. He probably would have been more likely to let Giancana help than Kennedy."

"Why not Kennedy and the Justice Department?" asked Mike.

"Bobby was the one that drove the wedge between President Kennedy and Sinatra Senior because of Frank's mob friends. Bobby didn't want to have his brother's name sullied with mentions of the mob, even though JFK was, in fact, sharing a mistress with Giancana.

"Frank always insisted that the feds shouldn't have even been aware of the kidnapping. They found out through illegal wiretaps."

"So, what's that got to do with your *daughter's* abduction?" asked Mike.

"Sinatra knew people, both in the mob and in the FBI. As attorney general, Bobby was, on paper at least, the FBI boss, but J. Edgar Hoover, the real head of the FBI, hated the Kennedys and wouldn't lift a finger for them. He also hated Sinatra."

"So, what happened?" asked Linda.

"The rest of the story, as I know it, may be true or not. Bobby Kennedy was completely out of his mind at the time. His brother had been assassinated just two weeks before Frank Junior's kidnapping, so whatever offers of assistance he might have made actually came from Justice Department subordinates, not Bobby himself.

"Sinatra was determined to keep all of the authorities out of it. He negotiated the quarter-million-dollar ransom personally, but the illegal wiretap on his phone tipped off the FBI. It also, not surprisingly, tipped off the mob. If not for the wiretap Hoover had ordered placed on Sinatra's phone, neither the feds nor the mob would have known anything about the son's kidnapping.

"Hoover contacted Sinatra and demanded that the FBI get the credit for negotiating the ransom and the eventual arrest of the kidnappers. The son of a bitch threatened Sinatra with taking the story public if he wouldn't agree. This was before Junior was released. Frank Senior felt sure that if the story got out, his son would be killed."

"So, Sinatra Senior let the FBI participate in the ransom and return?" asked Tommy.

"What choice did he have? Hoover was a total asshole. When the kid was finally released, Hoover's guys brought him back to his father in the trunk of a car. He said Senior should just be glad to have his son back alive."

"Jesus!" said Mike. "Is all that true?"

"Well, it's public record that Frank Junior came back in the trunk of a car. I can't say why. It's also public record that the FBI captured the kidnappers and ended up putting them away. As for the rest of it …"

"So," said Tommy, "all's well that ends well."

"Not totally," said Palkot. "Hoover *let it slip* to reporters that the whole thing may have been a publicity stunt to help Frank Junior's career. The defense attorneys tried to use the director's comments to get the kidnappers freed, but it didn't work. They went to prison."

"So … bottom line?" asked Mike.

"Bottom line is that Frank Senior believed until the day he died that the FBI almost got his son killed. He said *privately* that he thought that would have pleased Hoover. He felt that the only way to have handled the kidnapping was to avoid all authorities and media."

"I take it you agree?" asked Tommy.

"I think Sinatra Senior was right. I was determined not to call anyone until I heard from the kidnappers," said Palkot. "Not the local cops and certainly not the FBI. I wouldn't trust the feds as far as I could throw them."

"They've solved a lot of crimes, including kidnappings through the years," said Linda.

"I can't argue that, but I think they're a publicity-hungry organization that has become increasingly corrupt. If everything turned out well with Molly and Leah, they would take the credit. But if something had gone wrong—and with them, I'm convinced it would have—they'd have blamed anyone but themselves," said Palkot.

"So, what happened next?" asked Mike. "You're not a celebrity like Sinatra. Do you have the kind of money that would make it worthwhile for a kidnapper?"

"That's just it," he said. "I've got less than ten thousand dollars in savings and there is no family money on my side of the family. Or Molly's."

"So, it doesn't sound like they were looking for a big payday unless they had you confused with someone else and took the wrong child," said Tommy.

"Yeah, but that doesn't make any sense. The kidnappers didn't screw up. My ex and I live over a hundred miles apart, yet they took Leah from her *mom's* apartment and called *me* in Atlanta. We never even considered that they had made a mistake. I finally convinced Molly to wait to hear from the kidnappers before doing anything else. We were both wrecks."

"I take it they called?" asked Linda.

"Yes, they called just after noon the next day," Palkot said.

"What did they want?"

"It was the craziest thing. Whoever was calling was still using the Darth Vader voice, but I could sense he or she was concerned about our daughter. Leah had done nothing but scream and cry since her abduction.

"Whoever had physically removed her covered her mouth when she was taken out the window, plus Leah must have been only barely awake, so she hadn't made much noise. But she hadn't stopped crying since, until, that is, they sedated her. I believe the people holding her were very concerned for her welfare."

"What did they ask *you* for?" Mike asked.

"This is where it got very weird. First off, they said they would be willing to have Molly come to their hideout, for lack of a better word, and stay with Leah while I did certain tasks for them."

"And ...?" asked Linda.

"I didn't want my ex to go. I figured if she saw the kidnappers, they'd kill her for sure, and Leah too. Molly insisted that if Leah were killed, she would just as soon be dead as well.. They gave us a half hour to decide and get some things together, and they would call back."

"So ...?" asked Mike.

"There was no talking Molly out of it. When they called back, Molly was told to get clothes and anything else she and Leah would need for a maximum of three days. They specifically asked that she bring some of Leah's toys. Fortunately, Molly had brought some of Leah's clothes and toys with her. She said it made her feel more optimistic about getting her back.

"She was to drive to a nearby park at eleven that night and to come alone. They said they would know her car. They would pull their car up near Molly's and flash their lights once and then twice more.

"Molly was to go to their car and get in the backseat with the things she had brought. The voice said they would be wearing masks and that Molly should not speak to them. We decided to do as they asked. It seemed like our best chance to get Leah back."

"So she went with them?" asked Tommy.

"Yes," Palkot answered. "Afterwards, Molly told me she had been given a note saying they were going to put a hood over her head while they took her to our daughter. Then they drove around for almost an hour. She had no idea how far they had gone. She was scared to death during the ride, but they took her to Leah."

"What did they have you do?" asked Mike.

"Now it gets really complicated. First, I will have to tell you about Mark Alan. I also should tell you that I don't have any money to pay you. The little bit I did have, I gave to Molly when she left for Colorado with Leah."

"I guessed as much when you told us you didn't think your daughter was being held for a ransom you couldn't pay," said Mike.

"The rest of what I have to tell you—about Mark and what happened the night of the shooting—I probably shouldn't get into if you're not interested in pursuing this. It could potentially cause you trouble and would surely be a problem for me."

"What do you mean?" asked Linda.

"I'm not so naïve as to think that the people who orchestrated this shooting would not be able to discover that I was coming after them and that you were assisting me."

"You see that as a problem?" asked Mike.

"I see it as life-threatening. I only came to you guys because of how you were able to find out the truth about the Michelle Simons murder. I see a lot of similarities between that and what's happening to us now."

"Greg, I think we need a day to talk about this before we give you an answer. Can we get back together tomorrow afternoon?" asked Mike.

"That will work just fine. Will three o'clock be okay?"

"Three it is. We'll see you then."

***

"Well, what do you think?" asked Mike as soon as Palkot left. "Is this something we should take a look at?"

"It's intriguing," said Linda, "but why is he coming to us rather than the police? His daughter and wife are safe in Colorado. They're out of harm's way."

"Two things, I imagine," said Mike. "He says he's the one who gave the weapon to Alan. If he told that to the cops, he would just be trading places with his friend."

"And the other?" asked Tommy.

"All that stuff about the Sinatra kidnapping. That was very strange. He seemed focused on the fact that Sinatra kept the police out of it and was able to get his son back, despite the FBI. I don't think he trusts the local police, and certainly not the feds."

27

"Do you think Palkot, or even Alan, know more than they're saying?" asked Linda.

"We don't know enough to even guess at the answer to that," said Mike. "He did say there's more. I'm going to suggest we tell him that we'll look into this for him but can't promise how far we'll take it. Of course, when he tells us more tomorrow, we may change our minds.

"If we do go forward after talking with him, Tommy, I'd like you to take the lead and track down as much as you can in the next few days. Then we can decide whether or not to go all in. In the meantime, Linda and I will continue with other cases."

"Sounds fine to me," Tommy agreed. "Let's remember that at this point, we're not getting paid anything for this. That can't go on indefinitely."

"You're right," said Mike. "but don't forget the Simons case has been worth a fortune to us in good publicity. Compared to what that publicity generated for the firm, Diane Morgan's money was nothing. If this turns out to be big, it pays for itself."

3

As Tommy entered his home from the garage, he was greeted with a warm hug from his wife Ann and squeals and hugs from his two young daughters, Abbie and Lisa. Over the past year, the Cevilli household had once again become his haven.

After the death of his first wife, killed in traffic by a drunk driver, Tommy's life had been a mess. After months of work with a therapist, Tommy slowly turned his life around. He had married Ann. Their two daughters completed the happy family.

Then, Ann's MS nearly derailed them. Now her new drug regimen had made life good again.

"Honey, you're not going to believe what happened at the office today," Tommy began.

Ann had been thrilled when Tommy's part-time job at the Atkinson Detective Agency became full time. He had found his niche.

"I'm not even going to try to guess," said Ann. "What happened?"

"Well, I don't need to remind you that the place is doing great because of all the publicity we got from the Simons case."

"And yet you are."

"I am what?"

"Reminding me. C'mon Tommy, what's going on?"

"You know, getting Keith Michaels off death row was something no one thought we could do. The case was airtight. Now, we've been asked to look into a case where a happy ending is even more unlikely."

"And what case would that be?" asked Ann.

"Mark Alan. The SunTrust Park shooter."

"Are you crazy? That guy was caught red-handed, leaving the scene of the crime carrying the murder weapon. I hope that whoever wants you to disprove that is paying the agency *a lot*," she said.

"Funny you should mention that. The guy doesn't have any money. He's no Diane Morgan," he went on, referring to the wealthy sister of the man they had rescued from death row.

"The shooter's friend, a guy named Greg Palkot, told us a very interesting story and we agreed to do some preliminary investigation for him. Mike, Linda, and I all agreed that if there were something to his story, the publicity we would get would more than make up for whatever time we put in," Tommy explained. "We'll decide for sure after talking with him again, tomorrow."

"Sounds crazy to me, but maybe lightning *can* strike twice."

"That's kind of what *we're* hoping for," said Tommy.

After dinner, Tommy began his internet searches. He was determined to find out as much as he could about Miguel Fernandez, Mark Alan, and Greg Palkot. He would do a little reading on the Sinatra kidnapping as well.

***

A little over twenty miles from the Cevilli residence, Mike and Linda sat in the den of their Indian Hills home having an after-dinner drink. The Voice filled the room.

"It's no coincidence that we're listening to Frank, is it?" asked Linda.

"No, it's not," said Mike. "I think he's the greatest singer that ever lived and, of course, our discussion at the office made him the obvious choice for our evening's entertainment."

"That was quite a story Palkot told us," she said. "You think there's anything to it?"

"Before listening to Palkot today, I wouldn't have bet a dime on the chance that Alan didn't do it. But … strange things do happen. Let's see what Tommy comes up with."

"It seems so quiet in the house with Mikey off to college and Anna spending more time with her friends and school activities than she spends here," said Linda.

The couple had been thrilled when their son was accepted to the Berklee College of Music in Boston. He also received a generous scholarship. They talked on the phone several times a week and Mikey seemed to be thriving; but the family missed him immensely.

Mikey's younger sister, Anna, was now a high school junior and turning out to be a beautiful young lady. Her grades were good and her popularity was soaring—without, it seemed, causing an increase in hat size. Mike and Linda were proud of their kids.

"I think Stoph likes the music as much as we do. Look at him tapping his paw," said Linda, pointing at the family's beloved golden retriever. His formal name was Aristophanes. Stoph too had a less than enjoyable encounter with Dr. Jerry Simons, having been shot with a tranquilizer dart on the night when Simons met his fate at the Atkinson home.

"I'm so glad Stoph survived that bastard Simons," said Mike. "We were all pretty fortunate that night, thanks to Mikey.

"It seems a shame to waste this Sinatra music," he continued. "Anna's spending the night at Becky's. How would you like to 'snuggle' right here on the sofa? I don't think Stoph will mind, and no one sets the mood better than Frank."

"I was kind of hoping you'd suggest that. So… Fly me to the moon. Or even to llama land …" So off they flew.

.

4

The dark-clad figure strode purposely across the parking lot just north of downtown Marietta. He was a very angry man. He had done exactly as agreed. First kidnapped the kid and handed her over to the old couple. He'd killed the Russian kid; then the baseball player from the roof of the nearby hotel—less than four hundred yards, a simple shot for him. After all, he had killed many men from distances over a mile. He had disposed of the weapon exactly as agreed upon, then gotten rid of the old couple who'd held Palkot's kid and ex-wife.

The killer was angry that the Russian couple released the two hostages before he'd gotten the chance to dispose of them as intended. There was nothing he could do about that now. It was his fault. He had slipped up and let the couple know that the "job" was done and he would be returning to "free" the hostages. He guessed the old couple somehow sensed he was going to kill the girl and her mother. They should have worried more about themselves.

He was even more upset now because he was being forced to jump through hoops to collect the second half of his $500,000 fee. The first half had been deposited in his Cayman account before the shooting. His account was untraceable and accessible to no one but himself.

He might have been willing to forgo the second half of the fee: $250,000 for a couple of very easy tasks would have been sufficient. But he didn't want word getting out that his rates had dropped. He did have other clients afterall.

His agreement with the men who hired him was that the second half of his fee would be deposited into the same numbered account. Now, he was told, he needed to meet with a representative of the general and he would be paid in diamonds. It seemed that the old military man had come into possession of a large quantity of uncut stones whose value, he was assured, far exceeded the amount he was owed.

The killer stood near the side door of the shuttered convenience store as the man approached. This sleazy looking, little acne scarred bastard was new.

Even here, in this deserted parking lot at this late hour, the killer knew there was still a possibility they would be seen. The scarred man whispered, "If you don't mind, let's go to my car.

I've got your diamonds there, and also some information about another job the general would like you to handle for him."

"Let's get this shit over with," the killer agreed. "I'm tired of waiting to get paid. I'm not so sure I want to do any more jobs for your group. The general is getting to be a real pain in my ass."

"When you see the job we've got for you, you'll sing a different tune," said Scarface, as the killer now thought of him.

When they got inside the man's car, he opened the console and brought out an envelope containing a large number of fine diamonds. The killer knew from experience they were worth far more than what he was owed.

"You know this is bullshit," said the killer. "Why should I be the one to have to sell these diamonds? Why can't the general or his men sell them?"

"It seems that the general may have overreached in securing these stones. His superiors are watching him and his associates for any sign of moving them. They don't think I'm capable of it, and aren't paying attention to me."

"Sometimes it pays to be an ugly little fuck," said the killer, "but you need to give me the stones you kept for yourself."

"What makes you think I kept some?" he asked, guilt written all over him.

"Because in addition to being ugly, you're also stupid." As he spoke, he brought out a silenced pistol and shot the man twice in the head. The killer hadn't known of the attempted deception, but there could be no mistaking that guilty look.

Reaching inside the dead man's jacket, he removed the envelope with a small number of diamonds inside. The killer noted that the stones were some of the better ones from the initial stash.

"Well, maybe you weren't completely stupid. But now you're a dead little fuck." He wiped down everything he had touched, then threw down a few small packets of crack cocaine.

"Just another drug deal gone bad," he said quietly to himself. "And I guess someone else will have to do that other job." With that, the SunTrust Park shooter disappeared

5

Greg Palkot was alone in his Atlanta apartment. Since his divorce from Molly, it would have been very unusual for him not to be alone. He had no local friends to speak of, nor had he dated other women. The sparsely furnished apartment, mostly courtesy of Goodwill, did nothing to improve his mood. Even if he wanted to bring a woman back here, he figured, she'd take one look and run.

Palkot left the Marine Corps short of the necessary twenty years required for a pension. He thought that the move might bring Molly back. He'd hoped they might even get remarried.

She did not come back. Then he thought perhaps the kidnapping, though he had nothing to do with it might bring them closer, but instead it made his ex-wife even more determined to stay away from him. *"Death and violence will always be around you,"* she had told him. Maybe she was right.

Palkot had never wanted to be anything but a marine. He had loved the twelve weeks of basic training at Parris Island, SC, and been the best in his class with a rifle. His instructors admitted among themselves (but never to Palkot) that he was one of the best they had ever seen. He had been highly recommended for the sniper training course.

Those next twelve and a half weeks of sniper training had been the most intense and exciting time of Greg's life. He would not have traded his time as a United States Marine for anything in the world.

November 2004, Fallujah, Iraq

This series of intense firefights was being called the Second Battle of Fallujah by both the military leaders in the field and the attendant media. Back in February and March 2004, there had been multiple incarnations of the enemy in the Fallujah area.

Saddam Hussein, though a tyrant and a despot, had kept relative order in this and other parts of his country. His sheer brutality kept the disparate factions at bay. Now that Saddam was gone, every possible kind of insurgent—al-Qaeda in Iraq (known as AQI), the Islamic Army of Iraq, the National Islamic Army,

Chechen insurgents and various other groups—roamed the area, killing at will. All were in or near Fallujah.

On March 31, 2004, four independent Blackwater contractors from the United States were attacked, murdered, mutilated and dragged through the streets of the city. Generals James T. Conway and James "Mad Dog" Mattis had had enough. The might of the U.S. military was turned loose against the Iraqi barbarians. Within a few weeks, the first battle of Fallujah resulted in the occupation of the city by U.S. forces.

Throughout the battle, the enemy used schools and mosques as both hiding places and missile launch sites—then cried crocodile tears when those same sites were attacked, causing large numbers of civilian casualties. *That's the way these crazy motherfucking assholes fight,* Greg Palkot thought at the time. He had been deployed too late to be involved in any but minor mop-up actions.

A few months later, the United States turned the city over to a CIA-created government that was as effective as one might expect a CIA-formed government to be. In other words, a total FUBAR.

Palkot was well aware that it had been this same CIA that gave Osama bin-Laden and the mujahedeen their start as they fought the Russians who had invaded Afghanistan. By arming and aiding bin-Laden's fighters, the United States, through the CIA, had trained and armed the very same people who planned and carried out the 9/11 attack on the United States.

Now it was November 2004, and the battle to recapture Fallujah was under way. *This is utter stupidity,* thought Palkot. He remembered stories of Vietnam and Hamburger Hill. Marines would die capturing a piece of territory during the day and then, retreating, cede it back at night. Then the next day, the marines would have to capture the hill all over again.

How fucking stupid is that? he thought; but this is war, it's us against them. *Fuck these al-Qaeda pricks!* Palkot was a marine, and he would do his duty. *Semper Fi!*

Palkot and his best friend, Mark Alan, were on a rooftop near the center of the city, covering for the men fighting in the streets below. Whenever they could, they would call in artillery or some other support unit to take care of the good guys below. They had to be careful not to do too much shooting or their location would be discovered. If that happened, they would be forced to relocate quickly or be discovered and attacked.

Both had done their share of shooting. Alan was nearly as good as Palkot and they formed a formidable team. Other military branches used their snipers in tandem with a spotter, usually another sniper who would spot and help target enemies to be killed. They could trade off as one man became tired and the shooter would become the spotter. The U.S. Marines believed that if you were good enough to be a sniper, then *be* a sniper. Two guys might work in the same area, but they were both shooters, not spotters.

Then the unexpected happened. An enemy fighter suddenly appeared on the rooftop Palkot and Alan occupied. Who knew his exact affiliation? He was an enemy with a gun, and he was about to kill Mark Alan. Before Alan could get his gun up, the enemy's head exploded, spraying brain matter and blood all over him.

"Jesus Christ, what a fuckin' mess!"

"You're welcome," said Palkot. Alan quickly wiped the bloody debris from his face and they went on with their jobs.

After the fighting eased, Palkot and Alan returned to their base camp. Both were badly in need of a shower and sleep. They had been fighting over twenty-four hours straight and needed the break. Before heading for their bunks, Alan said, "Thanks again for back there. My brains would have been all over the rooftop if you hadn't made that shot. I owe you."

"You don't owe me anything," said Palkot. "I have your back and you have mine, simple as that."

"I appreciate you saying that, but I'd be dead if not for you. I owe you my life."

"Well, I hope I never have to collect on that debt."

"Isn't this all incredibly stupid?" asked Alan, attempting to change the subject.

"What do you mean?" asked Palkot.

"It's just like my dad said it was in Vietnam. The fucking politicians send us here to fight but anything we capture, those dumb hypocritical bastards give right back to the enemy. My dad always said it was because of TV."

"I know it's a total goat fuck, but what does TV have to do with it?"

"Dad always insisted that war was not meant to be a spectator sport," Alan replied. "Vietnam made it just that with the networks showing all those flag-draped coffins every night on the evening news. It's no wonder the public turned against that war. Who wouldn't get tired of watching a parade of coffins while trying to eat their pot roast?

"Also, the fucking politicians imposed all kinds of stupid rules of engagement that made it impossible to fight and win a war. Dad always said you should try every possible form of diplomacy before going to war, but if you were going to fight a war, then fight the goddamn thing. But the politicians are such chickenshits that they give back everything the military gains. It's not any different this time."

"But don't you agree that Saddam had to go, and we had to get justice for Nine-eleven?" asked Palkot.

"Look, don't get me wrong. Saddam Hussein was one evil bastard, and the world's a better place without him. But there's nothing here to replace him. A CIA-formed government? Gimme a fucking break! You see how well that worked out. Here we are again."

Palkot agreed. "I don't know what the answer is. The politicians, well … playing to the cameras."

"You know," Alan went on, "the last time we got it right was in World War Two. Did you know that it was nineteen forty-four before our government even allowed a photo of a dead American soldier to be published? We lost a hell of a lot more men in that war than we have here, but at least we had a plan."

"I didn't know about that photo thing," said Palkot, "but it makes sense. The U.S. had enough of a fight against the Germans and Japs. They didn't need to be fighting among themselves."

"Right!" said Alan. "And the rules of engagement were to kill the fucking enemy. They started it, not us. We didn't get our shorts in a bind over civilian casualties. No one's in *favor* of civilian casualties. But in a war, shit happens. Especially if you're determined to defeat the enemy.

"Look at the firebombing we did in Germany and Japan, and then the nukes. Today the fucking politicians and news media cry over every accidental civilian casualty. And the goddamn assholes that we're fighting know it and hide their men and supplies in mosques and schools to *ensure* that civilian casualties occur. They carry on as though we're the barbarians and not them. We don't want to kill innocent civilians. I, personally, would prefer not to kill anyone ... but it's a goddamn war!"

"You know a lot more history than I do," said Palkot, "but I don't disagree."

"You want to hear another amazing story? Again, nineteen forty-four, the U.S. and Allied forces were rehearsing the D-Day landings. There were cliffs to climb in France, so our guys found some British cliffs, to practice the assault.

"During that practice climb, the allies lost almost a thousand men. Dead! If that story had gone public, our media would have shit their pants and insisted we let Hitler win—just give it to him. And the goddamn politicians would have gone along. I hate that those men died, but I would hate it a lot more if Hitler and Tojo had won."

"I hadn't heard that story."

"FDR was all right for a politician," Alan continued, "but the only guy on the Allied side who had any balls was Churchill. If it hadn't been for him, we'd all be goose-stepping and *Deutsch sprechen.*"

"Or dead."

Alan nodded. "Stalin and the Russians were just in it for themselves and wanted all of Europe as a prize after the war—not that they didn't deserve a share of the spoils, Stalin or no Stalin. They lost more than twenty million killed, way more than any other country."

"I'm glad you're around to educate me," Palkot noted.

"You know what a monster Stalin was, don't you?"

"Yeah," said Palkot, "if even half the things said about him are true, he was as bad or worse than Hitler."

"Well … did you hear the one about how it was discovered that Stalin was still alive? When Russian leaders found out, they sent an emissary to meet with him and beg him to come back and save the country. At first, Stalin refused but was finally talked into it. 'Okay,' he said, 'I'll come back on one condition: this time, no more Mr. Nice Guy.'"

"That's terrible." Palkot chuckled nonetheless. "I think we both need sleep. See you in the morning."

***

Now Mark Alan was in custody for a murder that Palkot knew for a fact he had not committed. *And I helped put him there,* Greg thought. He could not let this stand.

On the afternoon after their initial meeting, the Atkinson Agency had agreed to at least take a look at Alan's case. Greg couldn't blame them for being cautious-he wasn't paying them after all. But they seemed interested.

He told them the rest of his story and knew he would have to wait for the investigation to unfold. Tommy Cevilli was taking the lead. Greg could only hope that the investigation would be fruitful.

6

Tommy Cevilli had always been a baseball fan. As long as he could remember, he had cheered for the Atlanta Braves, sometimes in person but usually in front of his TV.

He'd had little choice. His father, Anthony "Big Tony" Cevilli, was almost fanatical in his love for the Braves. Tommy therefore had been to many games with his dad, including Playoff and World Series games—and, of course, the most incredible game ever: the night Sid slid.

The not so swift of foot Sid Bream lumbered around third base to score on Francisco Cabrera's hit ahead of a weak-armed, pre-steroid throw from Barry Bonds. The unlikely victory took the Braves from a looming defeat to the World Series in a matter of seconds.

Tommy feared the stadium might collapse from the deafening cheers and frenzied stomping by the crowd. Often, he'd hear his father say, "Just go to YouTube and search for the night Sid slid." Those who did would be rewarded with Skip Caray's memorable call.

Now, though, Tommy was in a bind. He wanted to find out more about the life of Miguel Fernandez than just the public relations notes provided by the Miami Marlins. He had to know *why* Fernandez had been killed, and *who*, if not Mark Alan or Greg Palkot, had done it. He had his work cut out.

As he started reading everything he could about Fernandez, he came across stories of the player's childhood in Cuba, but they were vague and short on detail. He wished he knew more. What was young Miguel Fernandez' life really like?

Miguel's Story: Childhood

It was June 2006 in Pinar del Rio, a small city of just over 130,000 in western Cuba. Like all of the island just ninety miles south of the United States, it was poor. Everyone knew that the only wealthy people in the entire island nation were Fidel, his family, and his close associates. It was important that everyone publicly appear to love Castro, because disloyalty to his regime would be brutally punished. People's real feelings about the man and his regime were best kept to themselves.

Eleven-year-old Miguel Fernandez was at the little baseball field near his home. He spent most of his days playing *beisbol,* either in the park or sometimes at the beach. Years earlier, before the Castro brothers and their revolutionary thugs had seized control of the country from Fulgencio Batista, scouts from the U.S. baseball teams used to come to the beach to watch the best of the young Cuban players.

Miguelito, as he was known ("little Miguel") named after his father, Miguel Sr., adored the game of baseball. Even at this young age, he wished with all his heart to someday play in the land of the *yanquis* in *Los Estados Unidos*, the United States. And for his age, Miguelito was the best baseball player anyone in this part of Cuba had seen since Tony Oliva had played on the same fields fifty years earlier.

Just last month, Miguelito got to meet Tony O, as everyone called Oliva. He had come to the island of Cuba to visit family members who still lived there. Tony had seen young Miguel play in a youth league game and sought him out.

"Young man," Oliva said, "you're going to be a great player in a few years when you fill out. You are much better than I was at your age." The boy was speechless.

Then the truly unbelievable happened. Tony O asked if he might come by and visit Miguelito and his parents at their home that evening.

It turned out that Oliva's father had been a cigar roller too—same as Miguel Sr.—and one of the best in his day. Oliva's family had been poor as well, even poorer than Miguel's, so the men talked about their lives, of hardships and triumphs, while they smoked cigars and drank rum.

Oliva told Miguelito's father that he saw a bright future for his son if he could get to the United States to play. That would be difficult, he said, because the Cuban government certainly didn't want its young athletes defecting.

Back when *he* left Cuba, Oliva told them, it was slightly easier. Oliva's family somehow obtained a visa for their son to go north to the states. Problem was, the visa was for a younger sibling.

The Tony Oliva that baseball fans came to know was actually Pedro Oliva; Pedro used the visa issued to his younger brother, Tony. Thus, Pedro *became* Tony. His brother was good, but not the prospect Pedro was.

That his listed age therefore was reduced by three years was a plus for the baseball scouts, who now had an eighteen-year-old prospect rather than a twenty-one year old. Years later, the player legally changed his name to Tony Pedro Oliva.

The night wore on with much laughter. Young Miguel could not remember a time his father had laughed as much. Oliva told of coming to the states speaking no English. He suffered a couple of years in the minor leagues before reaching the majors to stay with the Minnesota Twins. There, Oliva caught two lucky breaks. The first was Vic Power, a Hispanic star who took Oliva under his wing. He would drive Tony to the ballpark every day, since Tony didn't drive. Oliva had a fantastic rookie season and, incredibly, won the batting title in his first full year in the majors.

Power took it on himself to teach Tony to drive. Not long after, he regretted it. Oliva lost control of the car, jumped a curb and crashed into a house. Fortunately, no one was hurt.

"I bet those homeowners were pissed," said Miguel Sr.

"No," Oliva replied, laughing. "When they saw that it was me that hit their house, they just wanted my autograph. They were big baseball fans."

"I assume now you can drive," said Miguel Sr., when the laughter settled down.

"I can," said Oliva, "but I try to stay on streets where the houses aren't so close to the road."

Tony's second lucky break was a girl named Donna. She was a girl of thirteen who often babysat for the Powers' children. At that point, Tony was one of those "kids."

Speaking almost no English, still, Tony asked Donna for help. She worked patiently with him, teaching Tony the language. They spent much time laughing, hardly understanding one another. A big Barbra Streisand fan, Donna taught Tony how to say, "people who need people are the luckiest people in the world."

Little Miguel said, "I hope you married Donna when she got older."

"No," Tony explained, "it was never like that. She was just a young girl who wanted to help me. But she is one of the best friends I ever had. She's married to a surgeon and living in California now. She's very happy. She's closer to Barbra out there."

As the hour grew late, Tony reluctantly rose to leave. "Miguelito, I want you to work hard at everything: school for sure, but especially at your baseball skills. If you can get on the national team, you'll have a chance to travel to other Latin American countries. That might give you a chance to escape to America.

"And one more thing. Get someone to teach you to speak English. It will make your life so much easier when you get to the United States."

Miguelito promised he would work hard. The boy noticed that Oliva had said *when* you reach the United States, not *if.* Meeting Tony O made him even more sure he would play baseball in *Los Estados Unidos*. He vowed to be a star and make Tony O proud.

7

Tommy, Linda and Mike were in the conference room of the Atkinson Detective Agency.

"Tommy," Mike asked, "what do you think? Are you making any progress on the Fernandez shooting?"

"I have to say that I've found some very interesting things about Miguel. We all know he defected from Cuba at age seventeen while playing for the Cuban national team. They were playing in a tournament in Rio de Janiero, Brazil. I'm not exactly sure how he managed to get away, but he did."

"How did he get to the states?" asked Mike.

"First he went to the Dominican Republic, and then on to the US," said Tommy. "The details of his defection have always been hazy. It seems some major league scouts, or agents, may have helped."

"I wonder how they even knew about him," said Linda. "It's not like anyone from the states was doing business in Cuba."

"Remember, this was during the Obama years, when the administration thought that if we were nice to the Cuban government, they would ease up on their human rights violations. Obama even went to Havana and, in fact, saw the Cuban national team play in a game he attended with Fidel. I'm not sure if Miguel was still there or not, but Obama was known to have said how good he thought the Cuban team was. I'm certain that scouts had been visiting the island as well."

Seven Years Earlier

Seventeen-year-old Miguel Fernandez was in love. Not with a pretty young girl or with any of the older women who would flirt unashamedly with the young star; no, Miguel was in love with the city of Rio de Janiero, Brazil. Everything about this new love was dazzling and wonderful.

He and his teammates were given a scenic tour. In addition to the world famous beaches-Copacabana and Ipanema-the highlights were *Corcovádo,* the hunchback, the mountain with the statue of Christ the Redeemer overlooking the entire metro area, and *Pan de Azucar,* Sugar Loaf, the other scenic mountain overlooking the bayside area of Rio. The views were spectacular. Everywhere you looked was a picture postcard.

Miguel was the biggest star on the Cuban national baseball team. The team was in Rio to play in the Pan American baseball tournament—*el Torneo Panamericano de Beisbol.* Miguel and the rest of the team had been doing very well in the tournament, defeating Colombia, Ecuador and Venezuela.

In two days, they were to play for the championship in Maracaña Stadium against the Brazilian national team. Cuba was the heavy favorite but the more than one hundred thousand fans, sure to be cheering for the Brazilian team, were hoping for an upset.

Brazilians had only lately come to be baseball fans. Historically, they were fans of *futbol,* or soccer, as it is known in some countries. A half century ago, Pelé led the Brazilians to three World Cup championships, in '58, '62 and '70. The *Brasileros* were mad for *futbol* and for Pelé. He became a national hero.

Now these sports-crazed fans were beginning to enjoy *beisbol,* as the Brazilians called it. Miguel had been surprised to learn before the trip that Brazilians didn't speak Spanish as their national language but rather Portuguese. The languages were similar and the residents of Rio worldly enough that language was no more than a minor barrier. It certainly was no problem between a handsome young athlete and the beautiful girls of Ipanema and Copacabana beaches.

Each player on the Cuban team had been assigned a guard by the Cuban authorities. Miguel and a couple of the other stars each were assigned two. These watchdogs maintained a fairly loose leash but they were always within sight. When Miguel set out to enjoy the sights and sounds of Copacabana beach, the guards were close by.

In no time, Miguel became fast friends with two bikini-clad *Cariocas,* as the citizens of Rio were known, Natália and Maria. Both spoke a bit of Spanish and were familiar with the game of baseball.

They also were stunningly beautiful, wearing the thong bikinis, affectionately known as dental floss, which were prevalent on Rio's beaches. Actual dental floss would have been nearly as effective at concealing the physical attributes of Miguel's two new friends.

The girls coaxed Miguel into playing a bit of beach volleyball and *frescobol,* an intense paddle game played up and down the beach. A natural athlete, he excelled quickly at these two games, neither of which he had ever played before. Miguel was a hit with the *Cariocas,* especially Natália and Maria.

They decided—with the permission of his guards, of course—to take him to dinner that night at Mariús, a restaurant at the end of Copacabana beach. Miguel ended up loving the restaurant almost as much as the girls.

Before going in, Miguel and his two stunning friends had posed with the pirate statue just outside the front door. The pirate was unmoved by the young beauties perched on his lap. Miguel doubted that *he* would be so unaffected.

Outside the restaurant, Miguel had the sense that Rio was magical. They were opposite the beach, and a pleasant salty breeze was blowing in across Avenida Atlántica. The girls' hair and skirts were tossed deliciously by the wind.

When they entered the establishment and were seated, things only got better. Miguel's guards positioned themselves, one inside and one outside the restaurant, both perfectly willing to let him have fun. No game tomorrow, so no early curfew. Both liked Miguel a lot.

While the girls enjoyed a couple of *caipirinhas*, a favorite local cocktail made of lime, sugar and *cachaça* (a Brazilian liqueur similar to vodka), Miguel contented himself with a Coke.

There was no contenting himself, though, when it came to the food. He had never seen or tasted anything like it.

After first going through a sumptuous salad bar, Miguel and the girls returned to their seats. Then waiter after waiter brought large metal skewers with every type of meat and seafood imaginable to the table. They proceeded to carve whatever sized portion that you wanted onto your plate.

Miguel was so busy accepting more portions that he couldn't find time to eat. The girls showed him that by turning a card at his spot at the table over from the green side to the red, the servers would stop bringing food until he turned it back to green.

Being a star in Cuba, Miguel and his family always received preferential treatment in the local marketplaces; but he had never seen anything like this. Every bite was delicious. He ate until he thought he would explode.

After dinner, Miguel, Natália and Maria strolled along the patterned sidewalk adjacent to the beach, trying to walk off what they could of their meal—followed, of course, by his bodyguards. The Cuban was amazed by the hundreds of sidewalk vendors selling everything from jewelry and clothing to artwork and yet *more* food. Miguel and the girls couldn't even look at the food.

After a half hour of walking, the girls said with a giggle that they would like to come back to Miguel's room at the Copacabana Palace Hotel for a "nightcap." No innocent, he eagerly accepted their offer. *Madre de Deus!* he thought. Mother of God! He was not sexually uninitiated, but he had never been with two girls at once; and both of these girls were more beautiful than any of his previous partners. Alongside his sexual excitement, a plan was taking form in his mind.

Miguel took the guards aside. He told them the girls wanted to come back to his room, and that if the two men could afford them some privacy, the girls just might be persuaded to "entertain" *them* later on. He falsely told them the girls had commented more than once how good-looking they were.

After an hour and a half of a sensuously pleasant time with Natália and Maria, Miguel put his plan into action. Pretending to get a busy signal for room service, he told the girls to stay right there in bed, beautiful and naked, while he went down to the lobby bar for champagne. Wearing only a bathing suit, T-shirt and flip-flops, he went out to the hallway where the guards were waiting. From the looks on their faces, it was obvious they had been listening at the door.

"I'm going downstairs to get some champagne for the girls, and for the two of you, if you like. Room service isn't answering.

The girls said to wait five minutes while they freshen up, and then the two of you should go in so they can 'thank you' for indulging us," he told them.

"We shouldn't let you go by yourself," said one of the guards.

"Well then, which one of you wants to go to the bar with me and which one wants some of the greatest *coño* you've ever had?"

The two guards looked at each other. "You promise you're coming back?" the first guard asked.

Miguel laughed. "What kind of idiot would go off and leave two beauties like that?"

The other guard asked, "Five minutes, you say?"

"That's right," said Miguel. "I think they have something special planned for you."

The men gave each other sidelong looks and reached a silent agreement. "Okay. But you better come back," said guard number one.

"I will," said Miguel. "And I'll knock first."

Miguel went down the hall, took the elevator to the lobby, briskly made his way past the bar and kept going. With nothing but his wallet, which he'd placed inside his bathing suit, he went out to the street and hailed a taxi. "Leve-me ao consulado dos Estados Unidos," he told the driver in the carefully rehearsed Portuguese phrase, meaning *Take me to the United States consulate*.

He had memorized that phrase as soon as he heard that his team would be coming to Brazil. It was a good thing that his friends had told him Spanish wasn't spoken here; this particular driver didn't seem to know any of Miguel's native tongue.

He was also glad he'd heeded Tony Oliva's advice to learn enough English to get by. His parents had sought out an English-speaking neighbor and Miguel had worked hard to learn the language. When he arrived at the U.S. consulate, he would be able to make his wishes known.

The driver complied with Miguel's Portuguese request, and they headed for downtown Rio. Miguel hoped the girls back at the hotel wouldn't be in too much trouble. He had not breathed a word of his plan. As much as Miguel loved Rio, leaving it would be the defining moment of his life.

***

"Did Fernandez meet with Obama after he defected?" Mike asked Tommy, their conversation nearing its end.

"No. Remember, Fidel was still alive but had turned the presidency over to his brother, Raul. Obama didn't want to be seen gloating over the young star's defection. Besides, the Cubans had not stopped their human rights violations. It was an embarrassment to Obama. Miguel had *lots* of negative things to say about the Cuban government, though."

"Didn't that cause trouble for the rest of his family back in Cuba?" asked Linda.

"His family was quite fortunate," said Tommy. "The transition of power from Fidel to his brother, Raul, kept a lot of bureaucrats in the Cuban government busy just hanging on to their jobs. Most weren't even *doing* their jobs, and, of course, bribes were always welcome. Sound familiar?"

"Bureaucrats are the same everywhere, I guess," Linda sighed.

"You're right," Tommy agreed. "It did take Miguel over two years to get his family to the states. After some initial setbacks, he managed to pay the way for them to escape. They all live in the Miami area now."

"Havana north," said Mike, with a chuckle.

"That is the truth," said Tommy.

***

Miguel's defection went without a hitch. The taxi took him to the U.S. consulate where he announced his intention to defect on the grounds of political persecution. The officers at the consulate soon ascertained that Miguel was indeed a member of the Cuban national baseball team. Miguel stated that he wanted to play baseball in the major leagues of the United States, but the Cuban government would not allow him to leave. He was given temporary asylum by the U.S. State Department.

For the previous year, Miguel had been in secret contact with two scouts for American professional baseball whom he'd met during earlier international competitions. They had told him that if he could evade his guards and reach a U.S. consulate or embassy, his asylum was sure to be granted. Scared to death, Miguel still feared he might be turned away. Then what?

Upon hearing the news that asylum had indeed been granted, Miguel uttered a short *Gracias a Dios*. Thank God. He didn't know what the future held but was positive it would be better than if he had stayed in Cuba.

Miguel had no idea what happened to the guards that night or the girls he'd left naked in his room. Nothing bad, he hoped. In fact, the girls were released by the authorities. The Cuban government claimed they had been involved in the player's defection, but their assertions were dismissed after a half hour of interrogation by local police. Clearly, they had known nothing of Miguel's plans but were, rather, just two "innocent" fun-seekers.

The two guards, however, were not so fortunate. They too had been questioned by the Brazilians and likewise released. The Cuban government had not been so kind. Both men were sent back to Havana on the first available flight. In the ensuing months, they were tried for dereliction of duty and each given prison sentences of five years.

The morning after his escape, Miguel got in touch with one of the scouts, a man by the name of Pedro Soto. Soto used all of his back-channel sources to arrange the first part of Miguel's journey to the United States.

He was secretly flown to the Dominican Republic. From there, Soto and his friend Tomás Santos started the process of auctioning off Miguel's talents to the highest bidder. While they waited, Soto and Santos provided him food and shelter. Both knew their "generosity" would be well rewarded. The player signed a contract naming the two as his agents in any professional baseball negotiations, as well as for any future commercial endorsements.

The auction didn't take long. "Miguel, the Miami Marlins are offering you a signing bonus of one point six million. I think it's a great offer and we should take it," said Tomás Santos.

"You're telling me I'm a millionaire and I've never even played in the United States?" asked an astonished Miguel.

"That's right," said Tomás. "After paying Pedro and me our ten percent, you will still have almost a million and a half dollars."

"I say let's do it," said Miguel. By the next day, he was rich.

***

Two months after defecting, Miguel was playing for the Miami Marlins Double-A farm team in Jacksonville, Florida. In his first professional game, he homered and doubled. Miguel Fernandez had arrived.

Thanks to Tony O's advice about learning English, things had been easier than they would have been otherwise. Miguel was even able to help other Hispanic players with matters that were much more difficult for non-English speakers. All the other players liked and respected him. He was a born leader.

Miguel joined the Jacksonville team in July when the season was already half over. Nevertheless, Miguel led the league in hitting with a .387 average. Playing in just seventy-one games, he still managed to hit twenty-three home runs. Nobody had seen anyone like him in decades, if ever. The Marlins considered calling him up to the parent club in September, but decided to let Miguel finish the season in Jacksonville and then play for a spot on the major league roster the next year in spring training.

After two weeks of spring exhibition games in early 2015, any remaining doubts about Miguel Fernandez' baseball talents had vanished. He was hitting over .400 with seven home runs and was a sensational defensive player, throwing out runners who dared him to show off his arm from right field. Without question, he would be in the starting lineup when the season opened.

The Marlins even decided not to play the silly game of making Miguel play in the minor leagues until the end of April, which would have given the team one more year of contractual control. No, he was just too good. Miguel Fernandez had reached the major leagues.

8

November 26, 2016, was a day for which tens of thousands of former Cuban citizens had been praying for many years. Fidel Castro was dead. The fiercely religious former residents of the island of Cuba were sure that Fidel and Satan were now becoming intimately acquainted. Hell was where most former inhabitants of Cuba believed Fidel *should* be, and surely was. Cuban citizens of Miami took to the streets in celebration.

One of the most recognized and outspoken speakers at the rallies around Little Havana was Miguel Fernandez. He shouted into the bullhorn about how glad Castro's death had made him.

"El Diablo Fidel está muerto. Que Raúl pronto se una como su hermano en el infierno"—the devil Fidel is dead. May his brother Raul soon join him in hell.

The crowd cheered lustily at these words. Almost all of the attendees shared his sentiments—all, that is, but a few pro-Castro Cubans, who remained silent, noting who most fiercely rallied the crowd against their beloved former leader. That would be Miguel Fernandez. His words were swiftly passed along to Raul, who now ran the island in an equally ruthless, though less charismatic, fashion. He would certainly not be pleased.

Raul was furious when he heard about the rallies and Miguel's part in them. *"Hijo de puta!"*—son of a whore! "Fidel and I gave that ungrateful asshole everything he wanted," said the Cuban president. "He not only defected but now has to celebrate Fidel's death. I will show the world that nobody can get away with that kind of disrespect!"

In the months before his death, Fidel talked long and hard with Raul about Miguel's betrayal. He was obsessed with the young ballplayer. The former leader had a plan.

"Hermano"—brother—"here is what I think."

Fidel's plan was as devious as it was brilliant. It would not happen overnight, but would play out over the next few years. It had to. On his deathbed, Fidel made his brother promise.

9

The Cobb County, Georgia, courthouse and jail stood a block off the Marietta square. The jail itself occupied the below-ground level of the structure. Out of a total of ten cells, three were now occupied. The first two contained drunk drivers unable to post bail. The third was occupied by Mark Alan, the accused SunTrust Park shooter, to whom bail had not been offered.

Alan looked around him. All in all, not bad. The cell was ten by twelve with the usual furnishings: a cot with thin mattress, sink–commode combo, and one chair. Like every cell he'd ever seen in the movies.

Held without bail for almost a week, he was arraigned two days after Miguel Fernandez was killed. With the assistance of his public defender, Alan pled not guilty. It would likely be several months before he'd go to trial, charged with capital murder. The death penalty would be an option if found guilty. He knew he might never be free again.

Mark had no idea how he'd ended up like this. He had responded without hesitation to his friend Greg Palkot's urgent plea for help. Palkot's daughter had been kidnapped, Greg told him, but he refused to go to the police. His ex-wife, Molly, was also being held by the kidnappers—of her own volition. It was the craziest story he ever heard.

"How could you have allowed Molly to go with them?" he'd asked.

"We both decided it was best for Leah. I was against it at first but she insisted, so I agreed," was Palkot's answer.

His friend had been convinced that if they followed the kidnapper's instructions, both Molly and Leah would be released unharmed. He had asked Mark for help. The thought of saying no to his friend never occurred to him. He owed him his life. Even had the rooftop incident in Iraq not taken place, he still would have been there for Greg. When a friend asks for help, Mark firmly believed, you don't ask why, just where and when. Yet something had gone terribly wrong.

A Week Earlier

The instructions to Greg Palkot were precise. He was to enter room 803 of the Omni Hotel at the Braves Battery at 8:30 P.M. with a key card provided to him in a dead-drop. He would find a locked case on the bed: he was not to open it. If he did, his daughter and ex-wife would be killed.

He was instructed to leave with the case and travel by taxi to downtown Atlanta to the Ritz-Carlton Hotel and proceed to room 314, again with a key card provided. He was told to place the unopened case on the bed in that room and then leave. If he did as instructed, he would be reunited with Leah and Molly within twenty-four hours. Greg prayed that everything would go as scripted. It did not.

Greg arrived at room 803 of the Omni Hotel at 8:30 P.M. on the dot. His key card worked and he picked up the case on the bed. It was heavier than he expected, but he was not about to open it. He'd been warned and would do nothing to jeopardize Molly and Leah's lives.

Greg went down the elevator to the lobby. Mark Alan had remained just outside the hotel to watch for any sign of a problem. As Palkot neared the doors leading out to the parking lot taxi stand, Alan suddenly appeared.

"I don't know what the hell is going on, but all hell has broken loose outside. Give me that case and you head for my car. There aren't any taxis getting into the parking lot. I'll go out the side door and you can pick me up there. I've never heard so many sirens in my life. I'll try to find out what's happening while you get the car."

"Why are you any safer with the case than me?" asked Greg.

"Because nobody knows anything about *me* being here. If this has anything to do with the kidnapping, you're the one they're looking for, whoever 'they' might be."

Greg handed the case over to Mark and headed out to get Mark's car. He immediately noticed at least twenty police cars with lights flashing in front of the hotel. Cops were everywhere with guns drawn. *I doubt this has anything to do with me,* thought Greg. *Something big is going on.*

As he headed for the car, at least half a dozen police officers went right by him without a second look.

I was right. Nothing to do with me.

Palkot drove out of the parking lot and was approaching the side door where Mark was supposed to meet him. As Mark emerged from the door, he was immediately surrounded by at least ten policemen with guns drawn. Greg watched his friend forced facefirst on the ground, the case ripped from his hands.

Greg watched in horror as one of the policemen opened it. Was opening the case a death warrant for his daughter and ex-wife? He had no way of knowing. The police, obviously satisfied with whatever they found inside, cuffed Mark and hauled him to one of their cars.

As the police drove off with Mark Alan in the backseat, Greg realized he might never see what remained of his family ever again. He slowly and carefully drove away from the scene, having no earthly idea where he was going.

10

Mike, Linda, Tommy and Ann were enjoying an early dinner at the Marietta Diner. The establishment, less than half a mile from the agency office and even closer to the Big Chicken, was a group favorite. Mike wondered aloud how the place could produce so many fantastic meals twenty-four seven.

"Maybe we're better off not knowing," Ann said.

"They must have people in the kitchen with magic wands, or magic spoons." said Linda. "Who cares? Let's just enjoy our meal."

Mike knew dinner would have to be quick, since Tommy and Ann were paying a babysitter and it was a school night. "Tommy, what's new with the Alan case? Is it going to be worth it for all of us to get involved?"

"I wish I could say for sure," said Tommy, "but I'm not convinced. There's a ton of evidence against Alan, despite what

Palkot says. The chances of the killer being someone else are about as likely as, well, the possibility that Keith Michaels didn't kill Michelle Simons."

All four got a chuckle out of that, remembering they had combined to do the impossible to get Michaels freed from death row.

"I've been looking at a lot of things about Alan, Palkot and Miguel Fernandez," said Tommy. "I've discovered a good bit, especially about Fernandez. There may have been a lot of people who wanted him dead."

"Such as?" asked Linda.

"For starters, the Cuban government and the mafia," Tommy offered.

"No shit!" Mike sat up. "This is sounding interesting."

"Plus, I can't get an answer to how the police were so quick to arrest Alan outside the hotel. I don't know if they were looking for him or for the case with the weapon. It had to have been one or the other."

"I've been wondering about the quick arrest myself," said Mike. "No one else was even stopped for questioning. The police just grabbed Alan coming out the side door. I also find it very interesting that the weapon inside the case—proven to be the murder weapon—was wiped clean of fingerprints. Who does that and then carries the weapon away from the scene himself?"

"That *is* strange," said Tommy. "Did the police find any brass?"

"According to my source, no," said Mike. "There was no bullet casing found, either at the scene or on Alan. Palkot and Alan say they don't know anything about the weapon, the cartridge or the scene. Plus, I'm told, Alan came up negative for gunshot powder residue; but of course he would, if Palkot had done the shooting. There are more questions than answers."

"If you can wait just a few more days, I might be able to give you a more educated opinion," said Tommy. "Palkot got his ex-wife to agree to talk to me on Skype. That's tomorrow. I want to check out a couple of other things, including the quick arrest. Two or three days max and I may have some answers."

***

The next afternoon, Tommy reached Molly Palkot via Skype. On his screen, Tommy saw a woman who looked like she'd been through the wringer. Her eyes, bright blue, seemed weary.

83

"First," said Tommy, "I want to tell you how glad I am that you and your daughter are safe."

"Thank you," said Molly. "I was scared to death for Leah. Less for myself. Also, she's adjusting to the trauma better than I dared to hope. The therapist is amazed, it's been so short a time."

"I can't imagine what this ordeal has been like for you," said Tommy. "I've got two girls of my own."

"It was frightening," said Molly, "but once I was allowed to join Leah, it was better. If this had gone differently, at least, well, I would have been there ..."

"Is it all right if I ask you a few questions?"

"I'm fine with that."

"Okay," Tommy began. "Was there anything that occurred before your daughter was taken that, in looking back, might now seem unusual?"

"You mean, was I warned in some way that this might happen? The answer is no. I've tried to think—of anything, even something subtle—that might have alerted me, but no, nothing. I never saw anyone following us or who seemed out of place or anything like that."

"Would you have been likely to notice?"

"My ex-husband is military, as you know. He always cautioned me to be aware of my surroundings and to be careful in parking lots and places like that. I used to laugh, that he was paranoid and overcautious. From now on, I'll be the paranoid one."

"A little paranoia is never bad," Tommy said gently. "I understand from Greg that you heard nothing the night Leah was taken. Is that right?"

"It is. I hadn't set the alarm in our apartment—something I've been guilty of in the past but will never allow to happen again. When Greg called before dawn, I thought he was playing some cruel game. Then, when I saw Leah missing from her bed, I thought he might have taken her."

"I assume Greg quickly convinced you he was not involved?"

"Yes, that's true. At that point, in addition to freaking out, I wished that he *had* taken her. Obviously, he hadn't. He was as upset as I was."

"Greg told me the two of you agreed not to call the police?"

"I only agreed to that until he could get down to Columbus, and we would decide then."

"So after he got there…?"

"I was hysterical and wanted to make the call. Greg convinced me that we shouldn't, at least until we'd heard from the kidnappers. He told me they had assured him they would contact us the next day."

"You agreed to wait?"

"I did. Greg went on and on about Frank Sinatra's kid. I had no idea what he was talking about, but he seemed more in control of himself than I was, so I agreed to wait, at least until we heard from the people who had Leah."

"So … they called. What happened then?" asked Tommy.

"It was strange. We had Greg's phone on speaker so we could both hear. The caller was using a voice distorter of some kind and sounded like the CNN guy."

"CNN guy?"

"You know, James Earl Jones. He was the voice of Darth Vader in *Star Wars*, but I always thought of him as the guy who said *'This is CNN.'* Every time I watch a *Star Wars* movie, I always wonder what the CNN guy is doing there."

Getting back to the subject, Tommy asked, "What did the caller say?"

"Well, he made it obvious to us that Leah was having a hard time. I felt that the caller was concerned—for her. Before *any* ransom demands, the caller asked what kind of toys or entertainment would calm her down.

Then the kidnapper suggested I might come and stay there as a hostage *along with* Leah. I thought Greg was going to have a heart attack when he suggested that."

"What happened next?"

"I immediately agreed, despite Greg's objections. We were assured no harm would come to either one of us. I was told to get some clothes and toys for Leah, and enough clothes to last me three days."

"And you agreed?"

"Of course! I didn't care what Greg thought. If something happened to Leah, I would rather the same happen to me. Besides, the caller sounded sympathetic. He said there were some things that he needed Greg to do before we could be released, but the task didn't sound outrageous.

" I'm calling the person on the phone *he* but I'm not sure if the caller was a man or woman. Neither Greg nor I could tell the gender because of the voice distorter. Also, the kidnappers clearly knew we don't have any money. A monetary ransom was never mentioned. This was never about money, as far as I can tell."

"What do you think it was about?"

"I don't know and I don't care. Leah and I are safe. That's all that matters."

"What can you tell me about the people who held you? I'm sure you have some thoughts about them?" Tommy asked.

"I do know it was a man and a woman. I don't know which was the caller. They didn't let me see their faces but didn't mind if I heard them speaking. Neither sounded like Darth Vader. I was relieved that they kept their faces hidden. It gave me hope that, in the end, they would let us go."

"Do you have any idea where you were?"

"No. I'm pretty sure we were in a house. Leah and I were kept in one bedroom with the window covered. They brought us food in that same room, that had an attached bathroom. We were on the ground floor; we never went up any stairs. And I never heard any other voices or traffic. I think we were out in the country somewhere."

"Anything else?"

"They spoke with a very slight accent. Neither Greg nor I picked up on that when the caller used the distorter. I couldn't tell if the accent was Spanish or something else, maybe Italian, or something else completely. I even thought it might be Russian. It was subtle—their English was good. Oh, and I think they were married or at least in a relationship."

"What makes you say that?" asked Tommy.

"Just the way their conversation went back and forth. For example, when I got picked up, only the man was in the car. We were led to believe that more than one person would be present when they picked me up, but it was only one. He put a hood over my head so he could drive without a mask. He drove around for a long time and I thought he was doing that to confuse me as to where we were going, or that the place they were holding Leah really was a long way off. It turns out he was lost."

"Lost?"

"Yes. When we got to where they were holding Leah, of course I was only concerned with her. But I did hear a bit of the couple's conversation. She asked him what had taken so long. He said he'd gotten lost. She scoffed. 'What? I should have stopped and asked directions?' She just laughed and said, 'You? Ask directions? You never ask directions. You never read directions. You always take the longest way to get anywhere.' Like it was a longstanding joke."

"They don't sound that threatening."

"They weren't. They kept assuring us that we would be released unharmed. And we were. After two days, they drove us to a gas station and left us there. They kept us blindfolded until they drove away, so we never saw the car we were in. I could tell it was an SUV, but it could have been any model."

"Do you think they were the ones who physically took Leah?" asked Tommy.

"I can't imagine it. They were older and nowhere near nimble enough to go through that window with Leah without my hearing them. They would have made noise."

"Do you have any idea who else may be involved, who could have physically taken your daughter?"

"I'm sorry, but I have nothing other than my strong impression that the couple couldn't have done it. I never heard them talk about anyone else, and I was never aware of another person being there. They had telephone conversations with someone, but I have no idea with whom. In fact, that's how they found out they could release us."

"So they got that information by phone?"

"Yes. And we left almost immediately. They were in a hurry. I figured they wanted to get back to their lives."

"Has Leah said anything about the people who abducted her, or anything else about the whole ordeal?"

"No, and her therapist says she probably has little or no memory of the actual abduction. I think that's a good thing, and her therapist agrees. We're trying to make it seem like she just had a little vacation with mommy."

"Did the kidnappers mention the baseball player being shot?"

"No, nothing was ever said about that. You think there's some connection?"

"Yes I do, but no idea what that connection might be, other than that Greg was tasked to pick up the murder weapon at the hotel where the shooter fired his shot."

"Greg did tell me that much," said Molly.

"According to your ex, circumstances caused him to hand off the case to Mark Alan, who was quickly arrested and charged with the shooting. After you were released, did you and Greg talk at all about Alan?" Tommy pressed.

"A little, but I was mainly in a panic to get Leah and me as far away from there as possible. I know that Mark was arrested for the shooting and that Greg insists he didn't do it, but that's all he would tell me. It's so stressful relocating and getting Leah to counseling that I haven't paid much attention to anything else."

"What do you think of Alan?" Tommy asked. "Do you think he's capable of murder?"

"I only met him a few times. He was a marine sniper, same as Greg, so of course he was capable of shooting someone. But the few times I met him, he seemed like a good guy. The three of us got into some philosophical discussions about war and diplomacy. Mark and Greg felt that war should only be fought when all diplomacy has failed, but that if you fight, fight to win. I didn't hear anything from him that sounded cold-blooded."

"Did he strike you as someone with extreme political views or as someone with a mercenary streak—in other words, would he kill for money or his beliefs?"

"I don't think so. I never heard any wild political views from him, and he didn't seem at all concerned with money," Molly replied. "More than once, I heard him say that as long as he had a warm place to lay his head at night, he was happy."

Tommy had no further questions. "Molly, I want to thank you for taking the time to talk to me. I am so happy that everything turned out okay for you and Leah. I know Greg is tremendously relieved."

"I hope I helped. I'm not sure what you're trying to accomplish, but Greg said it was important that we speak. As for Greg, I love him but I can't be part of the whole marine thing. He may have left the marines, but the marines have not left him. Greg would not be Greg without the military.

"I don't have any idea about the ballplayer being shot. I'm positive Greg had nothing to do with it and I can't imagine that his friend did either.

"He's bound to reenlist or go to work for a civilian security firm of some kind. It's in his blood. I wish I'd better understood before we got married and had a baby. I wish him the best and I want him to be a part of Leah's life. But it will have to be on my terms, not his."

"I understand," Tommy said, "and thanks again."

Ten Days Earlier

The middle-aged couple was north of Charleston, South Carolina, the day after Molly and Leah's release. As per instructions, they pulled into the parking lot of the Waffle House at the exit near the intersection of Interstates 26 and 95.

Both were glad the ordeal of guarding the girl and her mother was over. They were not criminals; yet it had been necessary to do this job to save their son. His gambling losses reached the point where he'd been threatened with death. He pleaded with his parents. All they had to do was this one little job and his debts would be forgiven. What choice did they have?

The man they knew only as a voice on the phone and a hooded and masked man who had handed them a small, terrified child was going to meet them here. He told them he would be bringing their son. Sergei was held to make sure the couple did as they were instructed.

A lone man approached their car. They rolled down the window. "Where's our son?" the woman demanded.

"He developed a vision problem and can't join us tonight," the man in the parking lot replied.

"What are you talking about, a vision problem?" the woman's husband asked.

"It seems the bullet that went into his eye caused him to be unable to see. Or do much of anything else either," the man chuckled as he brought his suppressed pistol into view.

"Please," the man begged. "We won't—"

"I'm sure you won't," the man replied as he shot them both in the head, point-blank. Then the SunTrust Park killer got into his car and drove off.

11

Tommy Cevilli was at the kitchen table enjoying his second cup of coffee of the morning when Ann walked in.

"What's got you up so early?" she asked.

"I'm trying to decide what to recommend to Mike and Linda about the SunTrust shooter case. I couldn't sleep worth a damn last night, going back and forth in my mind."

"What does your gut tell you?"

"That Alan didn't do it, and neither did Palkot. But that's just my gut. I'm impressed with both Alan and Palkot and with Palkot's ex-wife after Skyping with her, but I have no real proof of their innocence, or any clue about who might be involved."

"Your gut has a pretty good record," Ann said, "but you should probably refrain from stuffing it the way you did at the diner the other night. A *bigger* gut isn't necessarily more trustworthy."

"Yes." Tommy laughed. "But that meal was so good. And the cake—wow!"

"You didn't tell me much about your conversation with Palkot's wife," Ann said. "I wish I'd been at home so I could have listened in."

Ann worked as a nurse at a large hospital in Alpharetta. She had been out of work for more than a year during the time MS took control of her life. For a while, suicide seemed like an option, but Tommy and their two little girls needed her, even in a diminished capacity. That need kept her going until new drugs restored her to a much healthier existence.

The death of Tommy's first wife, killed by a drunk driver almost ten years earlier had nearly destroyed him. Two years after the accident he met Ann while working as a computer software installer at the hospital where she was employed as a nurse.

At the time, Tommy was obsessed with his own misfortune, bereft of joy after his loss. Knowing that he had to get on with is life, he asked the pretty and charming young nurse out to dinner.

After a few dates, Ann realized she was very much attracted to Tommy. He reminded her of Dean Martin in his prime—certainly not with his singing, which was abominable, but with his easy charm and sparkle. He had Dino's curly hair and Italian good looks.

Tommy was worth pursuing, though any further dates were contingent on him seeking grief counseling. Ann wanted to see his smile more often.

Reluctantly, he started seeing an Atlanta therapist, Dr. Agnes Alegria, and the results were nothing short of amazing. Inside of a year, Tommy was a new man.

He insisted that it wasn't so much Dr. Alegria but rather Ann becoming part of his life that was turning him around. Their relationship flourished and within a year they were married. Then, after seven great years and two beautiful daughters, illness struck. When the new meds came along, Ann thanked God *that* difficult part of her life was past.

"I've got to say, I was very impressed with both Greg Palkot and his ex-wife," said Tommy. "The kidnapping story, while bizarre, is believable. I just wish I had some idea about who was responsible, and why."

"His ex couldn't help there?" Ann asked.

"She didn't have any idea who the people were. She said they spoke with an accent, but she couldn't even tell what kind. She said it could have been Spanish, or something different— maybe Italian or even Russian."

"Do *those* accents sound similar?" Ann wondered. "I've never given any thought to which accents sound alike."

"Why would you?" asked Tommy. "Anyway, our conversation didn't clue me in on anything except that I believe she's telling the truth. Most likely the couple were working for someone else. They don't seem the type to mastermind a kidnapping and murder. Also, Palkot's wife believes that it was someone else completely who abducted their daughter—she feels the couple were too old, physically."

"So what are you going to tell Mike and Linda?" Ann asked.

"That I, at least, keep working the case. Since we're not getting paid, I hate to suggest that the agency concentrate any more manpower or money on this. I have the time, so I think Mike and Linda will be okay with me working, at least a bit longer, on this matter."

"If anyone can do it, you can," said Ann.

***

After lunch, Tommy arrived at the agency office in Marietta. Mike had some big news.

"My source at Cobb County PD says they have all the closed-circuit TV footage from the Omni Hotel and nearby buildings. They have video of Mark Alan taking the case from someone in the lobby. They also have 'someone' retrieving the case from room 803 in the hotel and taking it down to the lobby. The film clearly shows that someone to be Greg Palkot, although the police haven't ID'd him yet."

"Did you give him up?" asked Tommy.

"No," said Mike. "But I did call Palkot and urged him to turn himself in. They would have him identified in a matter of hours anyway."

"Did he agree?"

"Yes. He's probably walking into Cobb police headquarters as we speak," said Mike. "My source also told me that the police department received an anonymous tip just minutes after the shooting, alerting them to the case the weapon was discovered in."

"Who was the source? Do they have any ideas?"

"No. My guy just says the caller saw a man with the case heading up toward the roof, and was suspicious. To me, it sounds like Alan—or actually, Palkot—was being set up. That call would explain why Alan was arrested so quickly. It was the *case* the weapon was in, not a description of a man, that got Alan arrested so quickly."

"So, Alan and Palkot are both going to be in custody, charged with murder or conspiracy to commit murder," Tommy concluded.

"That's the way it would seem to be heading. But there is some better news," Mike added. "The police were able to get camera footage of the shooter in the act from one of the other buildings. He isn't identifiable—dressed all in black, with a mask covering the lower half of his face. But from his height and build, it's obviously not Alan or Palkot."

"What's going to happen with them? Will they be released?"

"Unlikely. I think at this point, they'll both be charged with conspiracy to commit murder."

"How can they be charged when the video shows it clearly wasn't them doing the shooting?" Tommy asked, incredulous.

"Because Alan ended up with the weapon and Palkot had it in his possession moments before. It doesn't take much to charge conspiracy, and this situation is clearly in bounds for that."

"So where does that leave us with the case? Our thing was to get Alan cleared. Now we've got both Alan and Palkot likely to be charged."

"Well, I did play one card in our hand. I told Palkot not to engage a public defender until after speaking with me again. I have someone in mind to defend him, and Alan as well, if that's possible," said Mike.

"And that would be ...?"

"Our old friend Stan Reznick," said Mike. "I think he owes us. He was pretty successful before the Michaels case, but our silence about his impairment during the trial phase of that case saved him some embarrassment, at the very least, and maybe a large loss of business. From what he tells me, his firm is doing better than ever."

Mike was referring to the fact that Reznick had not been as involved as he ordinarily would have while managing the Michaels case. His wife was battling cancer—something she did not want made public. Reznick performed well in court, but his lack of oversight resulted in critical evidence being overlooked. Only thanks to Tommy's diligence in researching the trial transcript was that evidence found, buried in a forensic report.

Had Reznick discovered that information at the time, the outcome of Keith Michaels' trial likely would have been different. Tommy's discovery of the evidence after Michaels was already on death row would almost certainly have gotten Michaels a new trial.

That was made unnecessary by Jerry Simons, the real murderer of his wife, being recorded confessing to that crime (as well as others) by, once again, Tommy. Simons was killed—by Mike Atkinson in self-defense—mere moments after his confession.

None of the people at the agency faulted Reznick for putting his wife first. Reznick had genuinely appreciated the team's silence on that; now, though, it was time for him to show that appreciation.

12

Stan Reznick was surprised to see Mike Atkinson walk in.

"You know," said Reznick, "I raised the cost of parking in the building just to keep guys like you out of here."

That remark got a chuckle. From his very first visit to the attorney's office, Mike had been astounded at the high parking fee charged by the building owners, of whom Reznick was the majority partner. Since the Michaels case, the Atkinsons and the Reznicks had become good friends, and both men were always fast with a smart-ass quip.

"Well you damn near succeeded. It's a good thing your secretary validates the tickets. Otherwise, no one would *ever* come down here."

"Seeing as how you *are* here, I'm guessing you *want* something from me." Reznick smiled.

"How can you be so cynical?" asked Mike. "Just because my agency and I are responsible for probably tripling your already inflated revenues, you think I want something?"

"So … this is just a social visit? You *don't* want something?"

"I didn't say that," said Mike. "I *would* like your help in a matter that the agency has gotten at least marginally involved in."

"And that would be …?"

"To at least consult with the marine snipers accused in the SunTrust Park shooting."

"Jesus Christ!" exclaimed Reznick. "Don't you guys ever get involved in something simple? Like maybe the Lindbergh kidnapping or the JFK assassination?"

"And I'd like you to do it pro bono," Mike added.

"Why in the name of everything that's holy would I do that?"

"Because the last time you worked with us on an impossible case, you turned out looking pretty good. Like I said: it probably tripled your revenues."

"Those revenues just barely doubled," Reznick said with mock indignation.

"Then you can easily afford a bit of pro bono work. And there's a good chance your revenues could end up doubling again."

"Okay, tell me about it," said the attorney. Mike did.

***

Later that same afternoon, Mike, Linda and Tommy were at the conference table.

"Reznick has agreed to at least consult on the shooter case," Mike told them. "He didn't completely commit, and I can't say I blame him. We're on pretty shaky ground here. *We* don't think Alan *or* Palkot were involved in the shooting, but we have no proof. And we have no idea who the real shooter might be."

"That sums it up quite accurately," said Linda. "Can we afford to continue?"

"If the agency is going to stay involved, I suggest it just be me," Tommy said. "You two can continue on other cases and make some money. It makes sense for me to stay on it at least until Reznick and I can talk to Alan and Palkot. I'm the least experienced as far as investigations go, so my time is less valuable—"

"Cut that crap," Mike cut in. "You're a natural. Stop selling yourself short. Besides, I already told Reznick you're the point guy on this."

"I appreciate you saying that, Mike. I *want* to be an asset; and I do have some ideas about how to pursue this."

"Let's hear them," said Linda.

"I see two alternative scenarios. One involves the Cuban government, and the other is organized crime."

"The mafia?" asked Mike.

"It's one possibility. Rumors are that Fernandez owed a lot to some pretty shady characters. I don't know if it involved gambling or something else, or even if it's true," Tommy said, "but I intend to find out."

"That sounds interesting, to say the least," Linda agreed. "What about Cuba? Do you really think Castro's government could have something to do with it?"

"It's another possibility I'm going to check out," said Tommy. "I've heard that the Cubans were very angry about Miguel's defection as well as his paying to smuggle his family to the states. Then he rubbed salt in their wounds at some rallies

108

celebrating Fidel's death. I don't think it's an *im*possibility that the Cubans are involved."

"Don't you think that the police will look at those possibilities as well?" asked Mike.

"I get the impression from public statements that the authorities aren't much interested in looking beyond our marine snipers. I believe they would love to close this case and get the national media off their backs," Tommy replied.

"Then *we* may be Alan and Palkot's only hope," Linda said.

"There's something else." Tommy hedged.

"Well…?"

"Are the two of you familiar with the Lindbergh Act?"

"Funny you mention Lindbergh," said Mike. "Stan was just telling me about him—or rather his baby. But no, I'm not sure what that is."

"After the Lindbergh child was kidnapped and murdered, congress passed a law that made all kidnappings a federal crime. So it's a sure thing we're going to be seeing those blue windbreakers with the yellow letters," Tommy told them. "And I don't know if those folks would restrict their investigation just to Leah Palkot's abduction, or if the connection to the Fernandez shooting would take them down *that* road. I'm guessing it would."

"Remember this," said Mike, "the FBI loves to crowd out the local cops and take all the glory, anytime they can. It's in their DNA. If they can connect the kidnapping to the shooting, they'll use that connection as a supposed motive for Palkot, or even Alan, to hire the actual shooter. Then the case would be closed and their *investigative brilliance* would get the credit. It's an FBI wet dream."

"We have to find a way to prevent that from happening. In the meantime, we'll have to be careful not to be seen as impeding the investigation," said Tommy. "The feds get very upset if someone gets in their way. I don't mind *visiting* the jail, but I sure as hell don't want to wind up there. Ann would kill me."

"So," said Linda, "we proceed cautiously and have Reznick talk to Alan and Palkot, but stay out of the way of the local cops and the feds."

"Agreed. And I'll also follow up on the possibilities I mentioned," said Tommy.

"Just be careful," Linda and Mike said at once.

13

As Tommy entered from the garage into the kitchen, he was delighted to see his father, Anthony "Big Tony" Cevilli, at the kitchen table entertaining Ann and the girls. His dad lived close, less than twenty miles away, and the senior Cevilli loved to stop by.

Big Tony was indeed big. He had always reminded Tommy of Ben Cartwright from TV's *Bonanza*, complete with full head of wavy silver hair. He had kept his, unlike Lorne Greene, who had worn a toupee that was affectionately known as the "Silver Fox" by the rest of the cast.

"Dad," said Tommy, "I'm glad to see you. I was going to call you tonight, to get your take on a few things."

"What would those be?" his father asked.

"It can wait until after dinner," said Ann. "I'm making your dad's favorite, linguini with clam sauce, heavy on the garlic."

"I called about two hours ago to warn Ann I was coming, and to make sure there was enough for an extra mouth ..." Big Tony began.

An hour and a half later, Tommy and his dad reconnoitered in the den for an after-dinner drink.

"So, Tommy, what did you want to talk about?"

"As a matter of fact, it's about baseball."

The senior Cevilli was a nut on the subject. He loved everything about baseball, and had even dreamed he might one day play professionally, but high school had been his last foray into the game. "Those damn curveballs!" he'd always say. Tommy grew up hearing about them. "Why can't they just throw the damn ball straight? I don't care how fast ..." Tommy knew this lament by heart.

"I remember you talking about having met Pete Rose when he was a young player. I'm looking into the Miguel Fernandez shooting along with Mike and Linda and I think there may have been some gambling or other questionable behavior on Fernandez' part. What was that story about Rose that you tell?"

"Shit, Tommy," said his dad. "I know you've heard it before—Rose is a few years older than I am, and me and some buddies were in Cincinnati for a game against the Braves, who were still in Milwaukee at the time. We were waiting outside the clubhouse door at old Crosley Field to get some autographs when Rose came out. The Reds had blown the game late to the Braves, and Rose was pissed.

"I was, believe it or not, an innocent at the time. That day, thanks to Mr. Rose, I learned to string profanities together in ways I never imagined. Hell, I'd never even heard half of those words. Every creative curse I've ever uttered was inspired that day by Pete."

"Do you think Rose was gambling from early on?"

"I'd bet he was calling his bookie to get odds on which of his parents would change his soiled diaper. Rose *always* did whatever he pleased. He was a tremendous player on the field, but off it, he was a total asshole."

"C'mon Dad, what do you *really* think of him?" Smiling, Tommy had also heard this before.

"You know, Tommy, I was watching that show the other night—*Billions* with Paul Giamatti. You know he's Bart's son, right?"

"I guess I knew that." His dad was referring to Bart Giamatti, the baseball commissioner who banned Rose from the game for life and then died of a heart attack only days later.

"Well, a lot of people, including Bart's family, thought the stress of the whole Rose matter caused his death."

"I remember you talking about that, too," said Tommy.

"I had this great idea watching his son on TV. I imagined a movie or a play with Paul, playing his father, talking to Rose. Instead of suspending him, he would pull out a gun and blow Pete's brains out.

Paul, as Bart, is standing over Rose's body. 'I'm going to be dead in a couple of days anyway,' he says. 'At least I get to have a little fun before I go.'"

"Sounds like a can't-miss, Dad. Why don't you submit it to Lifetime?"

"Maybe I will. You never know."

"So, bottom line, you think Rose was gambling early in his career, even on baseball?"

"I never heard that for certain. But *I'd* bet on it," said Big Tony. "Gamblers gamble."

"Well, Dad, *you* can bet that I'm going to find out if Miguel Fernandez was a gambler."

"I'm guessing you and the Atkinsons are trying to help the sniper that everyone says did the shooting?"

"Yes," said Tommy. "And as you well know, things often are not what they seem."

14

In August 2015, Miguel Fernandez was enjoying a storybook rookie year. With the season more than half gone, Miguel was second in the National League in hitting, at .322. He had nineteen home runs and fifty-eight RBIs. Things could hardly have been better, but Miguel was troubled.

It had been difficult for him to stay in touch with his family in Cuba. His mother and father, Maria and Miguel, Sr., as well as his elderly grandfather, Roberto Fernandez, still lived in Pinar del Rio; and while the U.S. cell providers did not have roaming plans to call the island, land lines were reachable.

Yet, in conversations with certain old friends, it was passed along to him that the family repeatedly had their phones seized and lines cut. Miguel did speak with them over friends' phones, but they obviously were having a difficult time. The Cuban government was unhappy with Miguel, and his family was paying the price.

Miguel formally requested that his family be granted visas to come to the United States, but Cuba was not cooperating. His family members were not being granted *any* visitation rights.

Miguel also discovered that the money he attempted to send to them through the usual channels was being confiscated. He was lucky that he'd taken his father's advice and sent relatively modest sums at first. Yet maybe his luck was about to change.

Carlos Fuentes, one of the two guards responsible for Miguel at the time of his defection in Rio, had contacted him the night before. Miguel was amazed to hear from him—and pained to have learned the guards were sent to prison for allowing his escape.

Miguel agreed to meet Fuentes in the coffee shop of the Fontainebleau Hotel in South Miami Beach the following morning. Fuentes indicated over the phone that he could help Miguel get his family out of Cuba.

As Miguel entered the coffee shop, he spotted his old guard Carlos at a corner table. When Fuentes saw Miguel, he rose with a smile and proclaimed, *"Mi amigo,* my friend, it's so good to see you." He gave Miguel a huge hug.

Miguel greeted the man warmly. "Carlos, it's so good to see *you*. I'm sorry for what happened to you and Juan. How were you able to get out of prison?"

"I was able to escape in the back of a grocery van. I noticed that the gatekeepers never inspected the vans as they left. I don't know if they were just lazy or incompetent. Probably both. I got under some empty crates while the van was being unloaded and just rode on out."

"That's great," said Miguel. "Was Juan able to get out too?"

"He wasn't so lucky." A shadow fell over his face. "He tried a few weeks later, but the prison started paying attention after I escaped. He was caught and killed."

"That's horrible." Miguel shuddered. "I feel responsible for his death."

"No, you're not. No one else is responsible for what the damn Castros have done. They are pigs!"

"So, how did you get to the states?"

"I am very lucky to have a friend with a boat. He works for the government, but he is anti-Castro. If the government ever found out, he would be dead, like Juan. Anyway, he is often able to smuggle people out to international waters, where he meets up with a friend from Miami who can smuggle them the rest of the way here. I'm not sure how they manage to evade the authorities of both governments, but they do. It usually is very expensive, but since the man is my friend and he knew I had escaped from prison, he did it for nothing in my case."

"Do you think your friend could help my family escape?" asked Miguel.

"That's why I came to see you. It would be very difficult, since your family is constantly being watched, but I think he could do it. It would be very expensive, though."

"How much?"

"About two hundred and fifty thousand for the three of them. There are three, right?"

"Dios mio," whispered Miguel. That would be almost half what he had left from his signing bonus, and his salary as a rookie was decent but nowhere near what other stars made. That would come later. "Yes, there are three, and of course, I'll do it. What do you need from me?"

"I can get back to you in two days with the details. You're sure you can afford it?"

"It's my family! Just tell me what to do," Miguel replied. He wished he had saved more, rather than spending so foolishly.

"I'll see you back here in two days."

***

As Carlos Fuentes left the coffee shop, he pulled out his cellphone. "He went for it," he said in Spanish, as he was getting into a cab. "He totally believed me. I can close the deal in two days. I'm trusting you will keep your part of the bargain." The voice on the other end gave him the assurance he needed, and Carlos ended the call.

Fuentes felt bad for Miguel. Despite having spent time in prison for allowing the ballplayer to get away and defect, he still liked the kid. Carlos wished for himself there was some other way out, as there had been for Miguel. There wasn't.

A month ago, Carlos unexpectedly was taken from his cell, given decent clothes, and driven to the presidential office of Raul Castro. Raul awaited him, along with a military man in camouflage fatigues who also wore a camouflage eyepatch. Joining Castro and the old soldier was a third man, dark complected, with a birthmark on his forehead.

"I trust you are being treated well, despite your treasonous behavior in Brazil."

"Yes sir," said Carlos. "I have no complaints." He wasn't about to voice anything negative regarding the inhumane treatment afforded him and other inmates to *this* man.

"I'm glad you are enjoying your time in my prison. But how would you like to get out and be reunited with your wife and little son?" asked Raul.

Not quite believing what he was hearing, Carlos replied, "Of course, sir. That is more than I could ever hope for."

"You would have to do a little job for me first. But I am sure that it is something a man like you can handle," said Castro, with a condescending smile. "After all, you were responsible for allowing that son of a bitch Miguel Fernandez to get away and defect to the United States to play baseball. You might have heard he is becoming a big star."

"No sir," said Carlos. "Sports coverage is not very good in the prison." The remark earned a rare chuckle from Raul.

"You can take my word, he *is* becoming a star. You are going to help me to be compensated by that treasonous *puta*," said Castro.

"Tell me what I must do, and I will do it," declared Carlos.

"If you had been half as loyal in Rio, this whole thing would be unnecessary," said Raul. "You will now be able to make it up to me. And if you do the job, I will release your friend Juan as well. But if there is a problem with your actions, your wife and son will not fare so well, and Juan will stay in prison forever."

Carlos felt a combination of joy and fear; joy at the possibility of being free and able to live out his life with his family, but fear at what he would be asked to do.

"I will do whatever you ask."

"I am going to give you tonight to spend with your wife and son," Raul told him. "A little taste of what freedom feels like. My men will, of course, guard your house, but I promise they will not listen at the bedroom window. They will bring you back here tomorrow morning and then my friend, the general here, will tell you what your task will be."

The night had been wonderful. Carlos could not believe he had spent the night in the arms of his wife, Diana. He and his son, Jose—they called him Pepe—had played and talked for several hours, and Carlos relished every minute. When his son at last had fallen asleep, he and Diana made love with an intensity they hadn't felt since their honeymoon.

When Miguel Fernandez' defection happened in Rio and he and Juan were taken into custody, Carlos was sure his life was over. When he and Juan entered the bedroom and saw the beautiful naked girls, all four were taken by surprise. The girls were expecting Miguel; the men—at least the bachelor Juan Escobar—believed the girls were waiting anxiously for them.

Carlos regretted going into that bedroom from the moment it happened. He would not have touched the girls, though he was sure Juan would have done enough touching for both of them. He loved Diana and had always been faithful; he really had no good answer as to why he hadn't stayed with Miguel, other than that the player had been so insistent.

By the time they had recovered their senses and realized what Miguel had done, he was gone. *Gracias a Dios*—thank God—that Diana believed his truthful retelling of the events in Rio when he was allowed to speak with her at the trial. Now he might once again have something to live for.

In the morning, Diana clung to Carlos when it was time to go. "Promise me that you'll do whatever is necessary to come back to Pepe and me. *Prometeme.*"

"Lo prometo, I will come back to you," Carlos promised, not knowing what Castro and the general would ask of him and hoping he could do the job and return to his family without also losing his soul.

It turned out the job was not as hard, or soul-wrenching, as Carlos feared. He had only to journey to the United States in a manner arranged by Castro, and spin a little tale to Miguel about getting his family out of Cuba. Castro kept a close watch on the remaining Fernandez family, and was not about to let them out of his country. Carlos, though, felt sure that God would forgive him for his lies. His family's future was at stake.

***

As Carlos left Castro's office, General Guillermo Gonzalez smiled. *Una mas retribución para los putos Americanos!* One more payback for the whore Americans! The general's thoughts drifted back half a century, to a place known as *Bahía de Cochinos:* The Bay of Pigs. As a young lieutenant in the Cuban army, and a favorite of his hero, Fidel Castro, Gonzalez fought fiercely to prevent the invasion of his island by the United States and that dog, President Kennedy.

The invasion had been thwarted, and there was only a bit of mopping up to be done. The *putas* from the United States who did not die here on the beach would spend the remainder of their lives rotting in cells.

Then, after all the fighting seemed to have ended, a shell exploded near Gonzalez. He would always remember the searing pain of the shrapnel burning into his left eye. The memory of that never left him. Many an American would pay for his lost eye— and that included the *cabrón*, Kennedy.

General Gonzalez self-consciously touched his eyepatch as his thoughts returned to the present. He chuckled as he thought about his patch. The very first bandage to cover his destroyed eye had been fashioned from his own camouflage shirt. He had never thought about using any other material to cover his wound. He knew that people called him *Camojo*—Camouflage Eye—behind his back. He often pretended to be offended, but in fact he wore the moniker like a badge of courage.

"I am an old man. This may be my last chance to hurt the whore Americans," he said to Raul. "I will make it count."

He turned to the dark-skinned man with the birthmark. "My friend, we have a lot of planning and work to do."

15

Stan Reznick was seated in the Cobb County jail conference room provided for meetings between prisoners and their lawyers. Reznick arranged to have this preliminary meeting with both Mark Alan and Greg Palkot, even though technically he represented neither. Stan knew he owed Gene Sanders, the Cobb DA, a huge favor for allowing this meeting.

Alan, of course, had been incarcerated since his capture outside the Omni Hotel the night of the shooting, now ten days ago. Palkot had surrendered just two days ago. His image on the closed-circuit television was unmistakable. He had wanted to remain free to help his friend, but he had no choice but to turn himself in.

After introductions, Reznick began. "Let's get down to business, gentlemen. I really should be speaking with you individually, but I don't actually represent either one of you, and

Tommy Cevilli told me that your stories are identical. So let me hear from you first, Mr. Alan."

Mark Alan proceeded to relate what happened to him from the time he was contacted by his friend, Greg Palkot, until the time of his arrest. As he began to tell Reznick what Palkot told him about his daughter's kidnapping, Reznick interrupted.

"Mr. Palkot, why don't you take over from here. Tell me about your daughter's abduction and your actions going forward. I'm assuming that what Mr. Alan has told me so far jibes with your account of the events related to the shooting and kidnapping."

"Everything he told you is correct," said Palkot. He went on to describe how his daughter was taken from his ex-wife's apartment and the events that followed.

"So you both assert that you had nothing to do with the murder of Miguel Fernandez and that as far as you both knew, you were only acting to secure the release of Mr. Palkot's daughter and ex-wife," said Reznick.

"Right," said Alan and Palkot simultaneously.

"That's a hell of a story," said Reznick. "If what you're telling me is true, someone went to a great deal of trouble to frame Mr. Palkot for Fernandez' murder, and you, Mr. Alan, were just in the wrong place at the wrong time."

"I was helping my best friend. I'd do it again. I did nothing wrong," said Alan.

"I'm not suggesting you did," said Reznick. "But this is quite a story. Do either of you have any idea who the real shooter was?"

Alan and Palkot looked at each other. Both shook their heads no. At last, Palkot said, "It would appear that *I* was the one that they—whoever *they* might be—intended to frame. I'm a former marine sniper living in the Atlanta area. I don't think this is anything directed at me personally. This was all about Miguel Fernandez; I'm just a pawn in the whole affair. For Mark, it's even worse. He was just helping a friend and is now charged with murder."

"Didn't either of you recognize the type of case the weapon was in, or have any desire to open it?" asked Reznick.

"It was not any kind of standard issue rifle case. It never occurred to me that I was carrying a weapon," said Palkot. "I think Mark would agree. The weapon was broken down and wrapped in bubble wrap, along with the accessories."

"That's right," said Alan. "When the police opened it in front of me, I knew I was screwed."

"As for opening the case myself, I was specifically ordered not to," said Palkot. "For all I knew, I was being watched, or the case might contain a signaling device that would let the kidnappers know I had not followed their instructions. With the lives of Leah and Molly at stake, I wasn't about to open it."

"So," said Reznick, "to sum it up, neither of you had anything to do with the actual shooting. You didn't know you were carrying a weapon. Neither of you have any idea who might have been responsible, and have no idea why you, Greg, were the lucky guy to get framed; and Mark, you were caught up in this whole mess just helping out a friend. Does that nail it?"

"That's the way I see it," said Palkot. "But I did think of one thing just now while we were talking."

"And that one thing is …?" asked Reznick.

"About six months ago, following one of those horrible school shootings, I was interviewed by a local television station. I'd met the station manager at a social function and told him I was a former marine sniper. I usually don't talk about my military service but we'd had a few to drink and I didn't see any harm in it at the time.

"Anyway, this particular shooting involved a sniper. The station manager remembered me and called to ask if I would do a short interview. I wasn't crazy about the idea, but he told me he would let me see the footage and if I didn't approve, it wouldn't be aired."

"I take it that it *was* aired," said Reznick.

"Yes. It was about a three-minute segment and the reporter was respectful to the military while of course being sympathetic to the poor kids who were shot."

"I would guess that's how you got on their radar—whoever *they* are, as you say," said Reznick.

"Thinking about it, that very likely is the case," Palkot agreed. "Like I said, I usually don't talk about my time in the marines. It sure as hell seems to have been a mistake for me to shoot my mouth off like that."

"So, anyone could have seen you on TV. If someone had been looking for a sniper to frame, you'd just given them a great audition," said Reznick.

"Shit!" Palkot exclaimed. "I knew I shouldn't have done that interview. That set this whole thing in motion."

"If what you both are telling me is true, you can't blame yourselves for Miguel Fernandez' killing. You were just convenient fall guys. If they hadn't seen your TV interview, Greg, they would have found someone else to frame. That's assuming the interview caused you to be selected," Reznick pointed out. "It could have been someone else who knew you were a former sniper."

"So, what now?" asked Alan. "Will you be able to help us?"

"I have to talk to Tommy Cevilli, and also to my staff. But the short answer is yes. I think I can help you. I will be in touch very soon."

The two former marines thanked the attorney. Their futures were in Stan Reznick's hands.

16

Vincent "Vinny the Grin" Funicello was smiling. Vinny was almost always smiling, hence the nickname. Truth be told, you didn't want to come upon Vinny when he *wasn't* smiling. When Vinny wasn't smiling, bad things happened.

Vinny was huge: over six foot five and weighing in at nearly three hundred and fifty pounds. In his youth, Vinny had been a very good football player, having received a full scholarship to attend the University of Miami as a nose guard. After graduation, he had been selected in the third round of the NFL draft by the Cleveland Browns.

Two days into training camp in his rookie season, Vinny's career came to a sudden end when he tore up his knee making a tackle. Vinny was forced to find a new way to make a living.

Vinny's NFL signing bonus gave him a taste of the high life that he was unwilling to give up. Two of his cousins worked for the notorious loan shark, Sal Pettino, in South Miami. The cousins put in a good word for Vinny, and after his knee finally healed—as well as it was ever going to heal—he was hired as a collector for Pettino.

If a client was ever late in making his payment, Vinny would have a talk with him. He was very persuasive. Vinny let the person know how displeased Mr. Pettino was regarding the financial delinquency. He also let on that he would only be talking to that person once. If payments were not brought up to date within a week, Vinny would be back, and this time he would have nothing to say. Bones, if not heads, would be broken.

Vinny's talent at bringing force to the enforcer role got high marks from Sal Pettino. It wasn't long before Vinny was top muscle in the Pettino organization. He'd just turned thirty-eight.

When Sal finally retired—if you can call getting an icepick shoved through your right eye and into your brain *retirement*—Vinny became the main loan shark in South Miami. He figured he could always get another icepick.

Today, Vinny had no reason *not* to smile. His lucrative loan-sharking business in the southern end of Miami was flourishing. A lot of people needed money that banks were not willing to lend. Mr. Funicello, as he insisted his clients refer to him, was more than willing to loan them whatever they needed.

In this respect, Vinny was the most reasonable participant in the business. In another respect, he could be extremely unreasonable.

He insisted on repayment with, of course, a very healthy rate of interest. In the last week, the people who owed him were making their payments ahead of time. His guys had not needed to so much as bloody a nose.

A few weeks ago, Vinny had been very *unhappy*. That dumbass baseball player, Miguel Fernandez, got whacked on national television, and the ballplayer still owed Vinny two million dollars.

"That was a goddamn crazy deal I made with the kid," Vinny had told his young lieutenant, Pete Rosetti. "But I liked him and the Cubans really fucked him over. At least I'll still get paid. But I figure I could have gotten twice as much out of him when he finally paid me off. He wouldn't have wanted the baseball big shots knowing that he'd done business with me. He could have ended up suspended or even kicked out of baseball altogether."

Miguel had come to Vinny two years earlier. He told Vinny that the Cubans of Raul Castro's regime had conned him out of a half million dollars. They sent a man whom Miguel thought was a friend to tell him he could get his family out of

Cuba for two hundred fifty thousand dollars. Miguel had agreed, feeling certain it was not beyond Castro to harm or even kill his parents and grandfather.

"They gave me a price that I agreed to," Miguel had said. "Then at the last minute, the *putas* raised the price to half a million. I had no choice but to agree. All the while, they were just fucking with me. They never intended to help my family, they just wanted to steal my money to punish me for my defection."

"So, your family is still in Cuba. What the fuck am I supposed to do about it?" asked Vinny.

"I know you're a baseball fan. I see you at the games a lot. You know how good I am, and that in a couple of years I'm going to be making ten or twenty million a year. I just have to get to the salary arbitration years, not even free agency."

"So ...?"

"Here's what I propose. You loan me two hundred thousand so I can get my family to the states. My friends have found a man who will get them out, but he's expensive. Not as expensive as those phony assholes who just took my money, but still more than I've got."

"And why would I do that?" Vinny asked.

"Because as soon as I get to salary arbitration in three years, I'll pay you two million. If my family is not free, I can't keep playing. It kills me every time I go out there and realize that my parents and grandfather are stuck in Cuba because of that pig Raul and his brother, Fidel."

"I have no love for the Castros," said Vinny, "and I'm sure you will pay me if you're able, because you know what would happen if you didn't. But what if you get killed or hurt? How do I get paid then?"

"I'll get an insurance policy that will pay ten million dollars if I'm killed, or five million if I'm injured and can't play. That way you get paid, no matter what, and my parents will be taken care of too."

"Kid," said Vinny, "you know that is not how I do business. But I like you. Bring me the insurance policy, and we'll do it."

Vinny kept his word, but now Miguel was dead. Vinny knew he would be paid from the insurance proceeds. Miguel's family wouldn't dare not pay him.

Yet Vinny's plan to extort more money from Miguel was out the window.

The only member of Vinny's crew who knew about the insurance policy and the deferred payment plan was Pete Rosetti. The rest of the gang believed that Miguel had been making regular payments, and now that he was dead, the rest of the loan would go unpaid. Pete had an idea.

"Boss, why don't we let our guys spread the word that you had Miguel whacked because he wasn't making his payments? The punks that work for us don't know what's going on. It will put the fear of God in, and quite frankly, scare the shit out of all the assholes who owe you money. And the crew wouldn't dare fuck with us."

"I'm listening," said Vinny.

"I'll tell them I asked if you had the ballplayer whacked and you just grinned, and that I took that for yes. I bet we won't see a late payment ever again. If everyone believes you'd have Fernandez killed, even with all the crazy money he stood to make, no one will come crying to us about needing more time to pay."

"Fuckin' a, Pete. That's brilliant. Go ahead and ask me," said Vinny.

"Ask you what, boss?"

"Oh for Christ's sake! Ask me if I had Miguel Fernandez whacked."

Pete asked. Vinny grinned.

17

The morning after Stan Reznick's meeting with Palkot and Alan, Tommy entered the Atkinson Detective Agency through the front door and was greeted by a new face.

"Are you Tommy?' she asked. "I'm Amy. I'm going to be working here full-time provided that all of you like the job I do."

Linda had run a help-wanted ad in the local paper and after interviewing several candidates, she hired Amy. The young woman was an attractive blonde who gave off very intelligent vibes. Tommy liked her immediately.

"I have a feeling that you are going to fit in quite nicely," said Tommy.

Mike and Linda decided they also would retain Susie, the part-time secretary who was pursuing her degree in criminology; they liked her too much to let her go. They hoped she might someday become an investigator with their little company.

After a few minutes of chatting, the three partners got down to business.

"Tommy," Mike began. "You were going to talk to Reznick by phone after he met with Alan and Palkot. What did he have to say?"

"The first thing he said was that you were lucky to have a friend like him. Someone who would perform legal services pro bono for which he would normally charge three hundred bucks an hour."

"Also, that he was going to order his secretary to no longer validate Mike's parking ticket for his office garage. It's the least you guys could do, he said, for free services. How much does he charge for parking?"

"You wouldn't believe it. Take my word that his garage will never be a homeless shelter," said Mike. "What did he have to say about the case?"

"He was quite impressed with our friends Alan and Palkot. He believes their story, that they had nothing to do with the shooting and were only trying to get Palkot's daughter and ex-wife released. He seems convinced he will be able to get the charges against both men dropped, but that it will take a while."

"Why won't they be dropped immediately?" Linda demanded. "It's obvious they're not the shooters, and the kidnapping gives them a perfect excuse for doing what they did with the gun case."

"There are bureaucratic hoops to jump through. He really hates that the FBI is involved, because of the Lindbergh Act. Stan areees the FBI is all about closing cases and getting all available credit and glory, local cops be damned," Tommy replied.

"As I said before," remarked Linda, "I've always seen them to be competent and hard working.

"I don't think Reznick would disagree," said Tommy. "He just thinks those at the top push the agents in the field too hard and are always way too happy to close a case. Another notch on the bedpost, so to speak. He sees it as *suits vs. boots*, and the suits are in command."

"So, who's the chief suit on this?" asked Mike.

"Stan says it's a guy by the name of Paul Randolph. He was a Comey hire, so ethics are not necessarily his strong point. For a lot of the guys Comey brought onboard, the ends always justify the means. Apparently, Reznick has had dealings with Randolph in the past; and he, according to Stan, fits that description to a T," said Tommy. "By the way, did you know

Comey loves being referred to as JC? It feeds his messianic complex."

"That's funny, but let's stick to the facts," said Mike. "Does Reznick think *anybody* in the FBI involved in the case might be a help?"

"Matter of fact, he mentioned a guy with the unlikely name of Bill Stoner," said Tommy. "He's the main field agent on this, and, according to Stan, who worked with him before, he's a straight shooter, a stand-up guy who won't cut corners or jump to conclusions."

"Then let's hope the boot has more influence than the suit," said Linda.

"We can only hope," said Tommy. "Stan feels they will press the Cobb County cops to keep both our guys in custody for the time being. I have to agree that would be best for now. Stan gave me the feeling that if Cobb released them, the bureau would find a reason to pick them up on charges related to the kidnapping and put them in federal custody.

"That would severely limit our access to them. In fact, Reznick was surprised the bureau hadn't pressed the Cobb authorities to release them for just that reason."

"Maybe the boot Stoner has more influence than we give him credit for," Linda suggested.

"Whatever the reason, I think it's best they stay in the Cobb lockup a bit longer," said Mike. "Are we in agreement on that?"

All agreed. Mike told the others that he would be calling Reznick to discuss strategy going forward.

"Meanwhile, Tommy, keep digging away at whatever angles you can find on Fernandez. Somebody other than Alan and Palkot killed him. Let's see if we can figure out who that might be."

18

Tommy ended his call and looked to Ann. "Mike and Linda are going to be interested to hear about this.".

"And what would *this* be?" she asked.

"That was Stan Reznick. He just got a call from the FBI agent running the Palkot kidnapping investigation. A couple was found murdered in their car near Charleston."

"What's that got to do with the kidnapping?"

"Remember my Skype session with Molly Palkot?"

"I do," said Ann. "I remember thinking how brave she was to give herself over to the kidnappers."

"It certainly was brave," Tommy agreed. "but nothing you wouldn't have done. Remember me telling you how Molly was instructed to bring clothes and some of Leah's toys for her to play with?"

"I guess so," said Ann. "Why?"

"The authorities found one of those toys jammed down the side of the backseat in the same car as the murdered couple. They're almost positive it was Leah's stuffed giraffe, since it had Leah's name tag on it.

Molly has identified it over Skype as being a part of her daughter's stuffed animal collection—her favorite, in fact. She called it *draffy* and has been asking for it ever since. Molly says she didn't plant it there. It must have slipped down the back of the seat and wasn't noticed."

"So, they think this pair were the kidnappers. Then who killed them?" asked Ann.

"Whoever was calling the shots. The couple was killed to cover the killer—or killers'—tracks, most likely."

"Did they identify the couple?" asked Ann.

"The FBI identified them as Ivan and Olga Kucherov. They were Russians who had lived in the U.S. since the early eighties. They lived just outside of Charleston, not more than twenty miles from where they were killed."

"What's known about them?"

"Not a great deal, nothing out of the ordinary. He worked as a housepainter. She was a waitress."

"That's all? They sound average, not like people who would be involved in a kidnapping."

"According to friends, they were both very nice. They have a son, Sergei, who reportedly has struggled with gambling. The bureau is trying to locate him to see what he knows, but so far, no luck," said Tommy.

"I wonder how this will affect the SunTrust Park investigation," said Ann. "What do you think?"

"We have a murdered baseball player and a murdered couple whose killings may be related. Alan and Palkot are in custody and unlikely to be charged with the Kucherov murders. They claim to have only been involved in getting Palkot's daughter and ex-wife back from kidnappers. Then a couple who *were* involved in the kidnapping, but most likely not the ringleaders, end up murdered. It's highly likely there's a good bit of head-scratching going on at the FBI."

"Nice summation," said Ann. "But what does it all mean?"

"It's a good possibility that one person killed all three."

"Well then, who? And why?"

"Who and why indeed. We have to find the answers ."

***

Mike and Linda indeed were interested in these latest developments.

"I think this is a good thing for Alan and Palkot," said Mike. "They couldn't have killed the couple; at least Alan couldn't have. He was in custody. And if Palkot knew who was involved in the kidnapping, he would have gone after them directly and not let Molly be taken; nor would he involve Alan.

"Whoever employed this couple likely murdered them to cover their tracks. That person or persons was probably involved in Fernandez' death as well."

Tommy and Linda agreed.

"That gets us the why of the Kucherov killings but doesn't explain Miguel's death. The big question remains; who?"

Ten Weeks Earlier

Miguel Fernandez rose early. He tried to get out of bed without waking his fiancée, Isabella, but failed. *God, she's a light sleeper,* he thought. Maybe subconsciously he preferred her to wake up when *he* did.

"You should go back to sleep, *mi princesa,"* said Miguel. "I have to be at the team bus for our trip to Port St. Lucie for our exhibition game against the Mets today, but there's no need for you to get up."

"Mi amor," said Isabella, pushing back the sheets and revealing her perfect unclothed body. "I would prefer to send you off to the bus with something to remember while you are at the game."

Miguel had met Isabella almost a year previously, and fell hopelessly in love. Not only was she beautiful, she was also smart, unpretentious, and seemingly unconcerned with Miguel's wealth and status as a baseball star. She hadn't even *been* a baseball fan when they first met, but she had fallen in love with this young player, now standing naked in front of her.

"Miguel," she said with a wicked grin, "I see you *are* interested in my offer. Do you have a flag to run up that thing?"

"Aren't you the sassy tart?"

"Tart?" she cried with feigned indignation.

"Would you prefer cupcake?" asked Miguel.

"*Cupcake* I can live with. I just hope you weren't thinking about some other woman to cause that reaction."

"Isabella," said Miguel, "you know very well that you are the only woman, besides my mother, that I ever think of. And thinking about my mother does not do this to me." He glanced mischievously downward and then into his lover's eyes.

"Well, then," she said, "come back to bed and let me show you how much I appreciate that I am the only *senorita* who makes that beautiful thing you have there point to the sky."

"Ay, Isabella," breathed Miguel, "I won't have any energy left for the game. I'll probably go hitless."

"Miguel," she said, "you won't have to do a thing. Just come over here and lie down. I will have a little conversation with him and make him feel better. He looks upset at the moment. I will have to get close enough so he can hear me whisper, but I'm quite sure he will enjoy what I have to say."

Miguel complied with Isabella's instructions and indeed, her whispers were more than enjoyable. Miguel thought momentarily about TV's *The Dog Whisperer*. Maybe his Isabella was a … the foolish thought was quickly replaced with sensations of pure pleasure. There was no room in his head for such *disparates*, nonsense. If he did go hitless this afternoon, it would be a very small price to pay.

"Mi amor," said Miguel, after Isabella had finished her ministrations. "I love you so much. I hate that before I met you, I was with many girls. If I had known that I was going to meet you someday, I never would have touched any of them."

"Miguel," she replied, "have you ever heard of Bread?"

"Pan?" he asked. *"Of course* I've heard of it. I often eat paninis."

"Don't be a smartass, Miguel. I'm talking about the old singing group, Bread. They had a song with the lyric, *'it really doesn't matter, how many came before, just as long as I'm the*

153

last.' That's how I feel about you. As long as I'm the last, what you did before makes no difference."

"Dios mio," declared Miguel. "I am the luckiest man alive. I love you so much. I promise there will never be anyone else."

***

Miguel hurried to make the team bus. He preferred to be early. He did not want anyone to think his success had gone to his head and that he was becoming some egotistical *cabrón* who doesn't care about anyone but himself. He was the reigning batting champion and MVP in the National League, but he wanted to remain the same man he had always been.

Here in the spring of 2019, he could not imagine life being any better. His parents and grandfather were safely and comfortably settled in the Little Havana district of Miami, not more than a short walk from Marlins Park, where he played half of the season's games. It was a rarity when any of the three of them missed a home game.

Miguel had arranged for his family to travel to several other cities around the league to watch him play, and more importantly, to get to see their new country. He felt very badly that they would not be able to go to Atlanta for the season opener.

His grandfather had just had a hip replacement and would not be able to travel for a few weeks. His parents would not have dreamed of going without the older man.

With the love of Isabella and the happiness of his parents, only one thing could make his life better: paying off the Vincent Funicello loan.

His agents, Pedro Soto and Tomás Santos, were in serious talks with the Marlins brass, and it seemed likely that Miguel soon would have a new contract—for hundreds of millions of dollars. He and Isabella and the rest of his family would never want for anything again. The children he and Isabella planned to have, and indeed their children's children, would be wealthy beyond anything Miguel could have dreamed as a boy in Cuba.

The agents hoped to have the contract settled before the start of the new season, but minor disagreements about how much would be deferred and for how many years the money would be paid out delayed the signing. Miguel's agents told him the documents should be ready for signing by early May, and that would include a large signing bonus. Then Miguel would pay back Funicello and his debt would be cleared.

Miguel's agents prepared him for the fact that the loan shark likely would ask for more money to ensure that none of the details would be made public. There was nothing illegal about the loan, but baseball looked sternly at any association with criminals. Miguel and his agents therefore decided to double the payout to Funicello before he even asked. That should ensure the transaction was never talked about in the *Miami Herald*.

Miguel went two for three in that day's game. Isabella had not sapped his strength. In fact, one of the hits was a long home run. *Dios mio, I love that girl. I can't wait to give her the ring.* His plan was to give her the engagement ring on the morning of opening day in Atlanta.

He had the good fortune of meeting a man named Ira, a jewelry merchant and also a dentist in Hallandale, north of Miami. Not only did Ira find the perfect diamond and design an exquisite setting at a remarkably good price, but he also did some fabulous dental work on his parents and grandfather, who bore the scars of Cuban socialized dentistry.

Come to think of it, I'll have to get Ira some tickets for the home opener, Miguel thought on the bus ride back to the Marlins training camp in Jupiter. *He has been a very good friend. He could have charged me twice as much for that ring. And my mother said she would never sit in any other dentist's chair as long as she lives. Maybe someday I'll even sit in his chair.*

Miguel, a major-league dentaphobe, shuddered at the thought. *Well ... maybe I* could *stand Ira's chair.*

19

Mike's conversation with Gil Torres of the Miami-Dade Police Department was informative. During his time serving on the Atlanta PD, Mike had developed a large network of acquaintances from police departments throughout the country, especially in the southeast.

Investigations often required cooperation between the police of different cities. Mike retained several of these relationships after moving to the private sector. Gil was one of them.

Mike had asked Torres what he knew about any connections between Miguel Fernandez and organized crime, especially gambling. Unpaid gambling debts had been the reason for more than one death of which Mike was personally aware; he figured that Fernandez made good money as a professional ballplayer, but he wanted to cover all possibilities. Who knows, maybe Miguel had even been banging some mobster's wife or girlfriend?

Mike wanted to hear what Torres had to say. The Miami police captain told him that as far as he knew, Miguel had not been involved with gambling of any kind, and he certainly had not been sexually involved with any crime boss's woman.

According to Torres' sources, Fernandez had been seriously involved with a girl by the name of Isabella Cabrera, a second-generation Cuban from Miami. He was not known to be one who jumped every woman who would hold still for him. His teammates described him as a terrific guy, the sort that the other players would be happy to have their sisters date.

"Don't get me wrong," Torres said, "he wasn't a monk. Before he got involved with the Cabrera girl, he dated a lot of girls. But we talked to several and not one had anything bad to say about him. I got the feeling that any of them would gladly have traded places with the Isabella. They all wished him well."

"Gil, I'm trying to find any reason that Fernandez might have been killed. You know I'm not a cop anymore, but my PI firm is involved in helping the two former marine snipers in custody. I'm more than ninety-nine percent certain that neither of those two guys had anything to do with the shooting."

"Who's paying the tab to you guys for the snipers? Has one of them got a rich sister?" asked Torres.

"No." Mike laughed. "Diane Morgan was a once in a lifetime occurrence." Torres was familiar with the Michaels case.

"We knew these two didn't have any money, but the police, and then the FBI, were all too willing to just lock them up and close the case. Palkot and Alan came to us for help. We're looking at it because we strongly believe they've been set up."

"I don't suppose you'd mind the publicity, especially if you help solve another high visibility case?" Torres asked, knowingly.

"Of course we wouldn't!" said Mike.

"I wasn't suggesting a low ulterior motive," said Torres, defensively."Just busting your chops."

"I know that Gil. I just wish we had something to go on. We know the Cuban government was not happy that Miguel defected, but that was five years ago. I'm looking for any possible criminal involvement."

"There was one small item on the radar that we looked at and dismissed," said Torres, "a rumor that Fernandez owed money to a loan shark, Vincent Funicello. The story was that Miguel had to borrow from the shark to get his parents out of Cuba."

161

"Didn't he get a huge bonus for signing with the Marlins? Why would he have to borrow money?"

"As I said, I don't think it was anything," Torres told him. "Fernandez did get a large bonus. Even if he *had* been in debt to Funicello and behind in his payments, my sources say he was about to sign a huge contract. You don't kill a guy who's about to come into a couple hundred million. You wait for him to get his money and *then* collect. So I don't believe Funicello was involved."

"No, not likely," Mike agreed. "Gil, I'd appreciate it if you let me know anything else that comes across your desk concerning Fernandez. I would also love to talk to his girlfriend, if she's willing."

"We've talked to her, and she is devastated. I'll ask her if she's willing to talk to you, since your firm is trying to find out who killed Miguel. I'll let you know,." Torres ended the call.

Just then, Tommy came in.

"Hey," Mike said. "I just talked to my source in Miami. It looks like gambling had nothing to do with Miguel's death. He said there might have been a loan shark involved, but it's thin."

"That's interesting," said Tommy. "Stan Reznick just called while I was on the way over. He heard from the FBI that they found the Russian couple's son, Sergei Kucherov."

"Good," said Mike. "What did he have to say?"

"About as much as you could expect from a guy with a forty-five-caliber hole through his eye."

"Shit."

"I second that. It appears, though, that gambling *was* involved with *his* death. Sergei was in debt to a Russian gambling syndicate that operates in Charleston. He'd been beaten pretty badly a couple of times for not paying on time, so speculation is that the Russians got tired of continually having to send their bone-breakers, so they killed him."

"Anyone in custody for the killing?" asked Mike.

"No," Tommy answered. "Those Russian mafia guys are too smart. No one has ever been able to pin anything on them, and this time's no different. The feds may well have decided that this fit their idea of what happened, but I think this time they may be right."

"So … what about the parents and the kidnapping? What are the chances that the whole family is murdered at the same time with no connection?"

"This just keeps getting more and more puzzling," said Tommy."We need to find some answers."

"I agree," said Mike. "I'm not sure where to go next. I'm hoping to talk to Miguel's girlfriend, but we're running out of leads."

"Something will come along," said Tommy. "It always does."

20

Bill Stoner was pissed. Paul Randolph was pressuring him to force the Cobb County DA to close the SunTrust Park shooter case by charging both Mark Alan and Greg Palkot with first-degree murder and conspiracy to commit murder. Their supposed motive was the kidnapping of Palkot's daughter. According to Randolph, killing Fernandez was what the kidnappers had demanded to get Palkot's daughter and ex-wife back alive, and Alan had assisted his friend in getting revenge for the kidnapping.

Stoner was sure those accusations were bullshit. According to Randolph, the Kucherovs were forced to kidnap Leah Palkot and, in turn, force Leah's father to kill Fernandez to eliminate their son's gambling debts. Then—in retribution— Palkot, aided by his friend, Mark Alan, killed the elder Kucherovs and their son, Sergei.

There were several problems with this story. First off, who forced the Kucherovs to do the kidnapping? Stoner felt sure that whoever had been responsible for that was far more likely to have killed the couple. Second, how had Palkot and Alan discovered the identity of the kidnappers? Had in fact the Kucherovs themselves actually done the abduction? A housepainter and a waitress? Elderly? And the big question-- how would Fernandez' death help anyone?

Stoner was positive that Paul Randolph just wanted the glory of closing this investigation, no matter how dubious his theory. Stoner had worked several cases under Assistant–Director Randolph in the past, and knew him to be a sloppy investigator and a glory hound.

Randolph personified everything that Stoner detested about an organization that he otherwise revered, and to which he had dedicated his life. Randolph, to him, was the ultimate ass kisser in pursuit of advancement. *He must have had to stand on tiptoe to kiss that fucking Comey's ass,* Stoner thought, with an uncharacteristic smirk.

Stoner was venting to his wife. "That dumb bastard comes down here from Washington and thinks he can just force the case closed ..."

"Could he be right about all of it, Bill?" asked Sally Stoner, trying to derail her husband's rage.

"No way!" Stoner argued. "I'd stake my reputation on it! I don't believe Palkot or Alan killed anyone. I think they were set up to take the fall, but damnit, I have no idea who arranged it, or why."

Sally loved and admired her husband. She knew he was one of the good guys. Lately, the FBI had been involved in shady practices, mostly involving partisan politics.

The past several years had seen her husband's beloved employers go from unquestionably the best crime-fighting organization in the world to a perceived collection of partisan hacks fighting a political battle for individual glory and advancement. And, of course, future book royalties.

Congressional investigations of the agency only added to that dark view. Sally knew that internecine partisan warfare was making her husband sick to his soul.

"Bill … I know you've considered quitting the agency and going to work for a local police department. Do you think this might be the time?" his wife asked gently.

"No way am I quitting in the middle of an investigation—and we are in the *middle* of it, not at the end, like Randolph is trying to say. If I quit, those two marines are screwed. I just won't let that happen," said Stoner.

"Good," said Sally. "I would have been disappointed if you had been willing to quit before this case is solved. So … what now?"

"There are some people I want to talk to. I don't know if you remember hearing about the Atkinson Detective Agency last year, related to the Keith Michaels case. Michaels' sister and those investigators did the impossible in clearing him."

"I do remember something about that," said Sally. "But what—you can't involve them in an FBI case?"

"They're already involved," said Stoner. "The two marines persuaded them to look into the shooting. I'm going to have a chat with them, discretely and, of course, off the record. I want to see what they found."

"Well, I hope they have something for you; nobody wants to see the wrong guys end up in jail."

"Nobody—with the possible exception of Paul Randolph, that is."

***

Stoner was seated at the Atkinson Agency conference table. When Amy announced him to Mike and Linda, both looked surprised. The meeting—with Stoner, Mike, Linda and Tommy—would be off the record.

"Agent Stoner," Mike began, "I've got to say, I'm surprised to see you here. How is it exactly that we can help you?"

"It's more a case of me helping you," Stoner replied. "First, I have to tell you that I'm not here in an official bureau capacity. My boss, Paul Randolph, would likely have me fired just for being here."

"Why is that?" asked Linda.

"Please remember this discussion is off the record," Stoner continued. "I'm convinced that Randolph is not interested in justice in this matter. He only wants the case to be closed, as a result of the bureau's investigation, of course, With all of the chaos at the top of our organization, I believe he sees this matter as a stepping-stone for him to become FBI director."

"Is that likely to happen?" asked Tommy.

"Unfortunately, yes," said Stoner, "and if it does happen, it could be the end of the FBI. It would be a perfect storm, combining corruption, arrogance of command and a total disregard for the laws of our nation. I love this country, and this bureau, way too much to stand by and let that happen without doing everything in my power to prevent it … everything *legal,* of course."

"You believe it's that serious?" asked Mike.

"Certainly. After Comey and his gang, and all those scandals involving the abuse of power inside the FBI in an attempt to influence elections, people are fed up. Good people of all political persuasions want the FBI to be an honest, law-abiding, crime-fighting organization. With Paul Randolph as head, the FBI will be more corrupt and self-serving than ever, guaranteed."

"All right, Bill—is it okay to call you Bill?" asked Tommy.

"Of course," said Stoner. "First-name basis for all of us is fine with me if there are no objections."

"No objections," Tommy agreed. "So, Bill, what can we do?"

"I know your agency has been looking into the shooter incident on behalf of the two marines, Alan and Palkot. I have the impression you believe they're innocent, and I feel the same. I saw your work with the Michaels case, and I trust your ability to unravel this one. I'm proposing that we share information and try to get a true and just outcome for these crimes."

"You're willing to share FBI intel with us? Isn't that illegal?" asked Mike.

"As far as anyone is concerned, you are no more than witnesses in the investigation. You have spoken with Alan and Palkot; I'm here to ascertain that what they told you jibes with what they told us. In the course of our conversations, various details are bound to be shared, and we may get into related investigations, such as the Kucherov murders. I assume you are aware that the entire Kucherov family was murdered?" Stoner asked.

"We are aware," said Tommy. "We also believe that their murders *are* related to the Fernandez shooting, and that Alan and Palkot were *not* involved."

"I couldn't have summed it up better," said Stoner. "Why don't we spend a bit of time comparing notes and theories?"

Over the next hour and a half, the four discussed the case and the investigation from every conceivable angle. All were on the same page regarding the innocence of Alan and Palkot, and they shared the frustration of not knowing who was responsible for the killings.

"I plan to do some follow-up on the loan shark, although I'm almost positive it's a dead end. You just don't kill a guy who's about to fall into multimillions unless you're a complete idiot. I'll look at gambling as well, but that isn't promising either," said Tommy.

"Linda," said Mike, "why don't you talk to the girlfriend, Isabella? She will probably be more comfortable speaking with a woman."

"Of course," said Linda. "Hopefully she'll open up and give us something new."

"My plan is to find out everything I can about the Kucherov murders," Stoner told them. "That's where we might find the key to it all. And I have to drag my feet, as inconspicuously as possible, of course, to keep Alan and Palkot out of federal custody. If the feds get them, we'll have a much tougher time. If you guys have any connections with the Cobb County authorities, use them. We need all the help we can get."

"Will do," said Mike. "Let's get together again soon. Bill, let us know when it's safe to meet with us."

"I'll be in touch within a day or two." Stoner left.

At the sound of the door shutting, the three detectives silently looked at one another.

"Goddamn." Tommy whistled. "I never thought I'd see the day an FBI agent would come to us and offer help."

"I think he's one of the good guys," said Linda. "I hope he doesn't get burned by this."

"Time will tell, but I agree that he *is* one of the good guys," said Mike. "Meanwhile, let's hope that Stoner can keep this guy Randolph at bay, at least for a while."

21

The face of Isabella Cabrera filled Linda's screen: careworn, beautiful, tired and sad. The loss of Miguel had taken a toll.

"Hello, Isabella," said Linda, introducing herself. "Gil Torres from the Miami police gave me your contact information and said that you were willing to talk to me."

"Yes. Hello, Linda," said Isabella. "Mr. Torres said he thought it would be good to speak with someone with your agency."

"First, let me say how sorry I am about your loss of Miguel," Linda began. "I didn't know him, but I have heard from many people that he was a wonderful man."

"He was the most wonderful person I have ever known," said Isabella, as fresh tears began to flow. "How could they do this to him?"

"I'm so sorry, and I can't imagine how horrible this has been for you, Isabella; but the way you asked how 'they' could do this—it almost sounds as if you know who did it," Linda probed as gently as she could.

"Yes, I know! It was the *puta* Castros, Fidel and Raul. They hated Miguel for defecting, and then hated him even more, when he was able to get his family to the states."

"Have you told Gil Torres, or any other members of the police, how you feel about this?" asked Linda.

"*Of course* I told the police, both here in Miami and also up in Atlanta where Miguel was killed. They all treated me like a hysterical little girl, but I know what I know. And I know what happened just before Miguel was killed."

Isabella began to sob. "I'm so sorry ... Miguel was everything to me. We were going to be married and have a family. Now, he's gone ... I'll never see him again ..."

"Isabella ... what happened just before he was killed?"

One Day Before the Shooting: Isabella's Story

How much more wonderful could life be? Isabella and Miguel were in Atlanta, where tomorrow night would be the opening of the new baseball season. Going on the road with Miguel was something she had rarely done the previous season as their relationship grew; but Miguel wanted her here for opening day: he had a surprise for her.

"Miguel!" Isabella pleaded. "Please tell me what the surprise will be."

"Mi princesa," he pled back, "what kind of a surprise would it be if I told you in advance? Are you like this at Christmas as well? Come on, let's go downstairs to the coffee shop and get some breakfast."

They rode the elevator down to the lobby of the Peachtree Plaza Hotel, where the team was staying. The Braves' new stadium was fifteen miles north in Cobb County, but visiting teams were still using the same accommodations they had when the Braves occupied nearby Turner Field.

In the elevator, Miguel teased his lover. "I think you will probably like the surprise very much. I will give it to you tomorrow morning. Today we can enjoy breakfast and then I have to go with the team to work out at the stadium. I will be back in time for dinner. I'm sure we can find a good place to eat."

"I guess I'll have to wait until tomorrow morning then. Are you sure I am going to like the surprise?"

As they reached their table, Miguel answered, "Yes, I am sure you will love it." Just as he finished speaking, two men entered the room. Miguel looked at them in astonishment.

Juan Escobar and Carlos Fuentes approached their table. "What the hell are you two *cabróns* doing here?" Miguel demanded. "Juan, you're supposed to be dead. And Carlos, I trusted you, and you stole a half million dollars from me!"

"Miguel," Carlos said, "I am so sorry. If you will allow us to sit with you and your lovely lady for a few minutes, I will tell you what happened."

With fire in his eyes, Miguel grudgingly agreed.

"Miguel … I was forced by the Cuban government to do what I did. They were going to harm my wife and daughter if I did not do as they ordered," Carlos explained. "I was told to tell

178

you I escaped from prison and Juan was dead. He knew nothing of this plan. I believe they chose me because I have a family and Juan does not."

Miguel softened. "I didn't know about your wife and daughter. I understand now that you had no choice. And I am so sorry that both of you had to go to prison for allowing me to escape. You really did go to prison, I assume?"

"Yes," answered Carlos. "The government was furious. We're lucky we weren't shot. If Fidel had still been president, we likely would have been executed. Raul is a bit less insane than his brother; he merely sentenced us to five years in prison.

"Juan served his full sentence," Carlos went on. "We just met again a few weeks ago and were determined to come to you and explain what happened."

"Why would you bother?" asked Miguel.

"Because we like you a great deal and do not blame you for defecting; we would have done the same thing had we been in your shoes," said Juan. "But we also wanted to warn you."

"Warn me about what?"

"When I was brought to Raul Castro's office to be given instructions on how I was to trick you out of your money," Carlos stated, "there were two other men present. They didn't have anything to say that day. It was only Raul bragging about how he and his men would make you pay,"

"They did make me pay—to the tune of half a million dollars."

"Well, when I returned for my instructions, Raul was not there-just the other two men. They had plenty to say between them when they felt I wasn't listening. At the time, I had no idea what they were talking about. That's probably why they were not more careful in front of me.

"Well," he went on, "I saw one of those two men about two months ago. He was a Cuban general who wore a camouflage eyepatch. I was with my wife at a restaurant in Havana. He recognized me as an ally from the meeting in Raul's office years earlier.

"I believe he had been drinking for some time. I think he was usually a taciturn individual, but the combination of the rum and his recognizing me from Raul Castro's office loosened his tongue, for he said, 'Miguel Fernandez thinks he has outsmarted us by getting his parents out of Cuba. Raul would have let it be, but the stupid ballplayer had to insult Fidel in public when he died. Now Raul has a plan to finish off the asshole, once and for all.'

"The story was that Raul had told Fidel on his deathbed that you would be dealt with, but he was merely telling a dying old man what he wanted to hear. But after the publicity from the rallies, he swore to finish you."

"How does he plan to do that?" asked Miguel.

"We don't know," replied Juan. "but we wanted to warn you. We were lucky enough to be able to leave Cuba because the government has made it easier. We wanted to get to you before something happened."

"Well, it won't be so easy for that *maricón* to get to me here. The team has plenty of security, and I will even hire more for myself and Isabella, as well as for my family when I get back to Miami next week. Thank you for coming to talk to me. Again, I am so sorry that the two of you were sent to prison because of me."

When they got back to their room, Isabella asked, "Miguel, do you think we should be worried?"

"No, *mi amor,*" Miguel said. "That's just a bunch of shit from a frustrated old Raul Castro. He will be dead long before me. ..."

***

As Linda listened to Isabella's story, she wondered if the Cubans indeed were behind Miguel's murder. "What did you think of the story the guards told?" she asked.

"Miguel told me not to worry, but then …" Isabella began to sob again. "Maybe if Miguel had believed them …"

"Isabella," said Linda. "I don't know what Miguel could have done. No one could have possibly foreseen it."

"It was all so horrible. I saw it. And just that morning, Miguel had made me the happiest woman in the world …"

***

"Isabella. Wake up my love." Isabella awoke to find Miguel kneeling beside the bed. "My love, I know we have agreed to be married, but there has been something missing. It's time we change that."

Miguel took her left hand in his. He then slipped the most beautiful ring she had ever seen onto the third finger of her left hand.

"Oh Miguel. It's beautiful. This is the most incredible surprise."

182

"Just say you still want to marry me and I will be the happiest man on earth. I will love you as long as I live."

"Miguel, I love you with all my heart, and always will. Of course I will marry you."

***

Linda could not help but get tears in her own eyes. When Miguel had pledged his forever love, he had less than twelve hours to live.

"Isabella," said Linda, "I promise you that we will do everything we can to find Miguel's killer. I'm so sorry ... I hope God will give you the strength to go on."

After assuring Isabella she would keep her informed, Linda ended the call. *The boys are going want to hear about this!*

Mike and Tommy indeed were interested when they heard Isabella's story.

"Why hasn't this line been followed up on?" asked Tommy.

"That's a damn good question. I can't imagine why it isn't front and center in the investigation. We need Bill Stoner in on

183

this. He must have heard about Isabella's assertions. I'm interested in what he has to say," said Mike.

"I'll set up a meeting with Bill as soon as possible. In the meantime," Linda suggested, "I propose we channel all of our efforts toward solving this. I know it's not going to make us any money, at least not in the short term, but after listening to that poor girl this afternoon, I can't stand the thought that someone could get away with this horrible set of crimes."

"We have enough cash to be able to focus solely on this case, for a while, at least. I do have a few things I need to finish up before I come onboard." said Mike. "Tommy, I'm counting on you and Linda to make progress. Hopefully, Bill Stoner will be able to give us some help as well."

"Thanks for the confidence," said Tommy. "I appreciate that, and I promise I'll work my ass off for you ..." he looked at Linda, "and for Isabella. We're going to solve this."

"I hope you're right," said Mike.

22

The SunTrust Park shooter was enjoying himself at Gulfstream Park in Hallandale, Florida. He always enjoyed the horses, and he usually won more bets than he lost. He didn't have a *system,* as so many of his stupid friends claimed to have. He bet on his gut feeling after walking around the stables and observing the horses and jockeys. Today he was up several thousand dollars, sure that any of those morons with their systems would not be doing as well.

He had always liked Florida. The weather was great; nice and hot, the way he liked it. It reminded him of home. He spoke a half dozen languages, so the cultural diversity of South Florida was not an impediment for him.

He felt his cell phone vibrate in his pocket. Recognizing the number, he answered in Russian. *"Da. Chto teper?"*—Yes. What now?

"I have some very interesting information for you," the man said in Russian. "If you handle this correctly, there is no chance you will be implicated in your adventure in Atlanta."

"*Boshe moy!*—My God!—Not over the phone, you fucking idiot! In person! When can we meet?" asked the shooter.

"I can see you in a couple of hours. Where are you now?" the caller asked.

"That's none of your goddamn business," said the shooter. "Let's just say I am on the north side of Miami."

"Do you know the Tatiana Club on Hallandale Beach Boulevard?"

"Of course I do," the shooter replied.

"Good. Meet me there in two hours. I know you will love what I have to tell you."

"I'll be there, but if you fuck with me, I will cut off your sad excuse for a dick and shove it down your throat."

"My friend, did you really kiss your mother with that mouth, once upon a time?" the caller chided.

"Don't you ever mention my mother again or I *will* kill you. I'll see you in two hours." The shooter disconnected and decided he had time for a few more races. He was just five minutes away from the Tatiana Club.

He wondered what could be so important that the man would call him like this. Usually, there was very little contact with the people for whom he worked. Everyone kept a very low profile. *Well, I will know in a couple of hours.*

Two hours later, the shooter waited in a booth at Tatiana's. This Russian establishment served acceptable food and had good shows—and so many Russians now were living in this part of the city that the club thrived.

The shooter did not believe the man who had called was any threat. He was sure that the scar-faced idiot he had killed in Marietta, though sent by this same man he was about to meet, was acting alone when he attempted to kill him and steal the diamonds.

The Russian was a bureaucrat, a middleman, and his sort were all the same. He existed to do the bidding of the people in charge. As he finished the thought, the shooter saw the man enter the club.

He was good-looking, just under six feet tall, with a full head of black hair combed back from a handsome face. He was dressed in tan slacks and a dark green *guayabera.* He spotted the shooter and proceeded to join him in his booth.

"How are you, my friend?" asked the man in Russian.

"I am not your friend," said the shooter. "What is this all about?"

"So touchy. And here I am with information that I know you will be glad to receive."

"Just give me what you have, and maybe you will not share the fate of that asshole you sent to deal with me in Georgia."

"Ah, Ricardo. I figured you were the reason he never reported back to me. He must have gotten a bit ambitious and tried to avoid paying you. You know that we do not operate that way. General Camojo was very unhappy."

"You had never tried to pull shit like that before, or I would not be sitting here," said the shooter.

"When his body was found, he did not have any diamonds on him. I assume you got those before killing him."

"Yes, your debt is paid. But wherever you found that asshole, I suggest you look elsewhere for future employees. He actually thought he could rob and kill me. Didn't you tell him who he was dealing with?"

"He was young, and he was keeping two women. Camojo didn't think the kid would try something that stupid, but he also knew that you were more than capable of handling anything that came along. I guess Ricardo figured it was worth a try. Now he's dead, and both of his whores have been made to disappear. We won't be having any trouble from them."

"Okay," said the shooter. "Let's drink to dead assholes and whores." He poured each of them a healthy shot of vodka from the bottle on the table.

The shooter knew that the man and his bosses would have been just fine if Ricardo had killed him instead of the other way around. He kept those thoughts to himself.

"Can't you get some rum? I hate this shit," said the man.

"What kind of Russian are you? Drink your vodka like a man. Then we'll talk. I'm the one who should be drinking rum; my mother used to put it in my bottle when I was a baby. *"Russians and rum? What next? Italians eating mashed potatoes instead of pasta?*

After downing his vodka, the man spent ten minutes telling the shooter what had brought him to this meeting. After he departed, the shooter had a couple more shots and thought about what he had just been told. He laughed to himself. *Vincent Funicello, you are one fucked asshole.*

23

Bill Stoner stormed angrily into the office Paul Randolph was occupying at Atlanta FBI headquarters. Randolph was seated behind a large oak desk with a stack of papers in front of him.

"Tell me you didn't know about Isabella Cabrera's story," Stoner demanded. "You're the one who interviewed her the day after the shooting. You wouldn't let me go near her."

"What the fuck are you talking about?" Randolph shot back.

"I think you know damn well. Her story about the Cuban guards meeting with her and Fernandez when they as much as predicted their government was going to try to kill him. I know Gil Torres told you about it."

"You mean that little Cuban whore Fernandez was sleeping with? She has about as much credibility as a homeless junkie," said Randolph.

"You know what, Randolph? You really are an arrogant prick. Isabella is no more a whore than our wives. Well, at least I can speak for *my* wife not being a whore. I don't know about yours."

Randolph was instantly up from his chair and in Stoner's face. "Watch your mouth, asshole. You seem to be forgetting who's in charge here."

"Oh, you don't have to worry about that. I know you're the big man here, and that you'll remind me every ten minutes if you think I've forgotten. I know you love sitting behind that big fucking desk and aim to sit behind an even bigger one in D.C. But you're fucking with an official investigation."

"What the hell is that supposed to mean?" asked Randolph.

"You want this whole thing closed so you can put a phony feather in your cap and get yourself appointed Director," said Stoner, irate. "That would be a damn sad day for the bureau, but I guess it would suit your buddies."

"I should have your ass fired for insubordination."

"You do that. I'll make such a stink about your handling of the Fernandez investigation that you'll *never* have your name on the director's door."

192

"I'm suspending you right now. Leave your creds at the desk. Now get the fuck out of here, or I'll throw you out myself."

"Sure thing, you fat flabby fuck," said Stoner. "Any time you want to step outside or into a ring, let me know. I'm not going to hold my breath, though. The whole bureau knows you're a sack of hot air and shit."

As Stoner banged out of Randolph's office and deposited his FBI credentials, he wondered whether his wife would be proud of him or aghast. *Proud,* he decided; yes, she would be very proud.

***

Tommy put down his cell phone and announced to the room, "Stoner was right. Randolph didn't react well to his accusations."

"What happened?" asked Linda, before Mike could get the words out.

"Randolph suspended him. Bill, it seems, used language that would make any sailor proud, and cause his mother to wash his mouth out with soap. That's a direct quote," Tommy told them. "He did admit to provoking him a bit."

"How so?" Mike asked.

"It seems that he questioned Randolph's wife's character."

"Ouch. But now that leaves us without any FBI assistance," Mike pointed out.

"Maybe it won't. Stoner said the guys at work know what a self-serving prick their boss is. When Stoner told them he'd been suspended, they promised to keep him in the loop."

Mike considered this. "Stoner strikes me as a good guy. I have a feeling the agents he's friendly with are probably the same type. I guess we'll find out over the next few days."

Linda and Tommy both agreed. For now, they had to wait.

24

Pete Rosetti was startled. He walked out of Charlotte Peroni's apartment hoping he didn't look like a guy who'd just had his ashes hauled, though that's exactly what transpired.

Charlotte was Pete's mistress, going on six months and he still wasn't sick of her: a new record. Charlotte's body, and the "talents" she possessed, could keep a guy interested for a long time. Pete had a wife and three kids at home but always figured, *a man's gotta do what a man's gotta do.*

He loved his wife, Maria, *but let's face it,* he thought, *she's always busy with the kids and no longer cares about her looks.* She'd put on weight and seemed not to mind that Pete pestered her for sex much less frequently now.

The dark stranger came out of nowhere. "Let's take a little walk, Pete"—a slight accent Pete didn't recognize.

"And why should I take a walk with you?" asked Pete, trying to sound braver than he felt.

"Because if you don't, I'm going to blow your nuts off with the forty-five I'm holding against you. Charlotte wouldn't appreciate you nearly as much if I make a eunuch out of you."

Goddamn. This guy knows my name and Charlotte's. "In that case, I *will* take a walk with you, for Charlotte's sake, of course." Pete's gun was in the back waistband of his pants, and he knew he couldn't get to it before this asshole would shoot him.

"Pete, you're a funny guy. I like that," the man said as he led him across the street to a small park. They sat on a bench, out of earshot of any passersby.

"So?" Pete demanded.

"Be patient, Pete. I know you are a patient man. That's a big part of why we're having this talk. I know you work for Vincent Funicello, and I know you're a better man than he. You're smarter and tougher."

"Wow," said Pete. "You didn't have to stick a gun up my ass to compliment me. Your breath's not that bad."

The man pushed the gun harder into him. "Being smarter than Funicello doesn't make you all *that* smart. It just puts you above a baboon's IQ."

"I see you're done with compliments. So what is it you want with me?"

"Here's the way it is, Pete. Vincent Funicello is going to die. You can either join him, or you can help me arrange his trip to the great beyond, and in the process, give yourself a promotion. And, by the way, if Vincent finds out about our little discussion, you *will* die. Don't believe for one second that you can warn him without my knowing. So ... what do you think, Pete?"

"Even a baboon could figure that one out. What do you need me to do?"

The man laid out the plan for Pete. "Do you think you can handle it?"

"Yeah, no sweat. It's past time for Vinny to go."

"All right. I'll be in touch to give you the specifics." The SunTrust Park shooter walked away.

People really are stupid, the shooter thought, amazed. *How the hell would I know if Pete told Funicello the plan? Like I got a lot of Italians working for me!* He was depending on Pete's ambition. *Funicello is as good as dead.*

***

Vinny the Grin was living up to his nickname. Everything seemed good these days. Pete Rosetti's idea about tacitly taking credit for killing Miguel Fernandez had helped business tremendously, at least the collection side. People weren't quite as anxious to take out new loans with him lately, but Vinny was sure that would turn around soon.

Rosetti and his crew spread the word about Vinny's supposed role in Fernandez' killing. The Cubans and the baseball fans weren't happy, but that was no big deal to him; no one was about to call the Better Business Bureau, much less the cops.

Pete said earlier he had things to go over with him that they couldn't discuss on the phone. *I wonder what the fuck that's all about?* Oh well. The guy was doing a terrific job making sure collections were up to par: real easy, with the Fernandez story out there. *I got Pete to thank for that. I might have to give the guy a little bonus.*

***

Tommy had been unable to find the two guards who met with Miguel and Isabella the day before Miguel was killed. Isabella remembered their first names only: Juan and Carlos. Bill Stoner, with his sources, found their last names. Neither, though, were able to find any trace of Juan Escobar or Carlos Fuentes.

For all Stoner and Tommy knew, the men may have been part of the plan to kill Miguel. Yet it remained unlikely that the guards would warn the target if they were part of the plot.

Stoner's government sources found no record of anyone with those names entering or leaving the country in the past thirty days. They were at an impasse.

"If it's like Isabella said, that the Cubans were responsible, then those two guys would be lying very low," Tommy pointed out.

Stoner and Tommy were meeting over breakfast at a new spot in Woodstock called The Maple Street Biscuit Company. When the manager greeted them, Tommy was vaguely aware he had seen her before, but couldn't remember where. It was bugging him.

"If it was the Cubans," Stoner replied, "there's a good chance the guards are dead. Raul's government has good intelligence and may have had the men followed. They would have seen Escobar and Fuentes meeting with Miguel and Isabella."

Tommy, snapping out of his earlier distraction, agreed. "I hope that's not the case. Certainly, it's a possibility. No bodies have turned up, but shallow graves are easy enough. We may never know what happened to those guys."

"Yeah," said Stoner. "This shooter doesn't leave loose ends. Palkot and Alan are probably lucky to be in custody. Even if they never laid eyes on the shooter, they could have ended up like the whole Kucherov family. They may still."

"What's your gut feeling?" asked Tommy. "You think this is all one guy?"

"It's hard to say. One guy *could* have done it all. It's not like the killings were done at the same time, hundreds of miles apart. But if it's not just one guy, I feel sure they are taking orders from the same boss."

"One thing all of us at the agency do feel certain about: Palkot and Alan had nothing to do with the shooting or any of the killings. I can't believe Randolph has convinced the Cobb authorities to keep them locked up," said Tommy.

"Paul is a piece of work. If he maintains any position of power in the bureau, you can bet I'll never work there again. And I think I'd be okay with that."

"I thought you *loved* working for the FBI?"

"I've always loved it," said Stoner, "but seeing what guys like Randolph have done to the agency makes me and a lot of others sick to our stomachs."

"Stan Reznick told me late yesterday afternoon that he's close to getting Palkot and Alan released. There's no evidence sufficient to continue to hold them. The kidnapping of Palkot's daughter gave them a perfect reason for doing what they did. They didn't break any laws. Unknowing possession of a murder weapon is not against any law I know of. It looks like your 'buddy' Randolph may not get his way much longer," said Tommy. "The cops will have to cut our guys loose."

"He'll fight their release to the end," said Stoner. "Then he'll find some other convenient solution instead of trying to find out the truth. By the way, I think Reznick is one of the good guys. But have you ever used the garage in his office building? You have to take out a second mortgage to park."

"No, I never did," said Tommy.

"You should probably start saving now."

As the two men prepared to leave, the manager came over. "How was everything, gentlemen?" she asked.

"It was fantastic, the food is terrific," Tommy said. "You know, I feel like I've met you someplace. You look familiar."

"I used to work in a dentist's office, Dr. Bob Hartman in East Cobb. Maybe you met me there?" said the manager. "I'm Blair, by the way."

"I'm Tommy, and this is Bill. I was in that office one time with Mike Atkinson. Does that name sound familiar?"

"Of course. He's famous from that Keith Michaels case, and he *was* a patient in our office."

"What made you change professions?" asked Tommy.

"I decided I'd rather be part of bringing people something they like—such as this great food—rather than sending them back to the dentist's chair. Dr. Hartman was great, but I see a lot more smiling faces here than I ever did there."

"I think you made the right decision," Bill Stoner smiled. "I'll be back."

"I look forward to seeing you. Bring your friends along too!" Blair waved them good-bye.

25

Mark Alan and Greg Palkot were free men. Over the objections of FBI Assistant Director Paul Randolph, the Cobb County District Attorney dropped all charges against both men and apologized for having held them in custody as long as he had. He informed both men and their attorney, Stan Reznick, that they still could have charges brought against them, although he did not speculate on what those charges might be.

They were not, however, protected by double jeopardy laws since they had not been tried in a court of law; the DA advised them, "keep your noses clean"—Randolph was on the warpath. Both pledged to walk the straight and narrow.

Now they were seated at the big conference table, along with Mike, Linda, Tommy and Stan Reznick. Mike opened the discussion.

"Stan, it's safe to say we all appreciate your efforts in getting Greg and Mark released and charges dropped. Where do you think they stand going forward?"

"We're going to have to watch out for Randolph," said Stan. "He has more arrogance and ambition than anyone I've ever met, and I've met my share of arrogant, ambitious sons of bitches."

"What exactly do we have to watch out for?" Palkot asked.

"You heard the Cobb district attorney tell you that new charges could be brought against you, including charges just like the ones that were dropped. That's what Randolph will attempt to do, but he'll make them *federal* charges. If that happens," Reznick explained, "the two of you will find yourselves in a federal lockup, with a lot less any of us can do to get you out."

"What other charges could he bring?" asked Greg.

"The only federal crime in any of this mess was the kidnapping," Reznick pointed out. "He'll probably attempt to charge the two of you with crimes related to that. He could try to find a workaround that would end up bringing weapons charges or something related against both of you. Then he could amplify those charges and you'd both end up recharged with conspiracy to commit murder, and maybe even the shooting itself, but by the feds-not local authorities."

"Could he actually pull that off?" asked Tommy.

"The FBI is a very powerful organization, and Paul Randolph is high up on the org chart. He will not take this defeat—and that's how he sees it—lying down. Someone in his position who doesn't give a damn about doing the right thing can do a lot of damage."

"What would you suggest *we* do?" asked Mike.

"Look, you guys aren't the FBI or police of any kind, but you all are damn fine investigators," said Reznick. "I'd suggest that you find out who is behind this and who pulled the trigger. It won't be easy, but you *will* have some FBI help, although Randolph won't know that. The reason Bill Stoner isn't here today is because he's meeting with some of the guys who are working the case. I should hear something from him late this afternoon."

"What about Greg and me?" asked Mark Alan. "Do we just wait around until someone comes to lock us up?"

"No," said Reznick. "I was about to get to that. Right now, there are no charges filed against either of you, and no one has ordered you to stay in the area. I think it would be a good idea if the two of you made yourself scarce. I'd suggest you not tell us where you're going and that you stay in touch with us with burner phones. Pick up a bunch of them at Wal-Mart."

"So ..." Palkot looked tense. "You're saying we should *hide out?*"

"You wouldn't be hiding out from any authorities, so there's nothing illegal about it. You'd just be unavailable to the FBI, or anyone else, on short notice. And if *we* don't know where you are, we can't be forced to tell anyone."

"The two of you can decide where you are going. It would be good if you checked in with us every couple of days," Mike suggested. "Tommy, why don't you give the guys your cell phone number? That would be a good way to contact us. Try calling in the evenings, say, after dinnertime, if you are going to make a call."

Tommy did so, they agreed to stay in touch, and then left.

"What are our chances, Stan?" asked Tommy.

"Impossible to say," said Reznick. "You guys might get real lucky and have the answers to all your questions drop in your laps; that's unlikely. It'll depend on how much time and resources you're willing to put into a pro bono gig."

"We'll talk some more about that," said Mike. "Meanwhile, let us know what you find out from Bill Stoner."

"I sure will."

After Reznick departed, Linda asked, "What do you guys think? Alan and Palkot are both free men, at least for now. Is there any reason why we shouldn't just chalk this up as a victory?"

"It doesn't feel right to walk away at this point," said Mike. "No one has paid the price for all of these deaths. Hell, there might be more dead that we don't even know about. I say let's stay on it, for a while at least."

"I was playing devil's advocate, you know." Linda blushed. "I feel the same way. Tommy?"

"I agree with both of you," he said. "We didn't get into this just for good press."

26

Almost six weeks had passed since the horror, and Isabella Cabrera finally found herself able to open up. Linda Atkinson and her partners seemed to be the only people who truly cared about finding out what had happened and why.

"It had been such a perfect, wonderful day," she said to Linda via Skype. "You know that Miguel formally proposed to me that morning ... the ring made it official ... more real ..."

"I remember you showed me the last time we spoke. It's beautiful," said Linda.

"Yes it is ..."

"What happened the rest of that day? You told me about the two Cuban guards showing up the night before. Did you see any more of them?"

"No. We didn't see them again. They told us their story and there was no reason for them to hang around. They knew they were also in danger."

"So, you never heard from them again, even after the shooting?"

"No, not to this day," said Isabella. "Are they okay?"

"No one seems to have any idea where they are. I think you know that several other people were murdered—also related to Miguel's killing," Linda told her. "The same thing may have happened to the guards."

"Oh, I hope not. They were nice men and seemed to care a great deal for Miguel."

"Tell me about the rest of the day," Linda gently urged.

"As I said, it was a perfect day. Miguel and I took a taxi to the stadium; since I was going to be at the game, that seemed best. When we got there, Miguel went into the clubhouse first to make sure everyone was decent, not changing into their uniforms. Then, when it was okay, he took me inside. Miguel wanted to show everyone my ring."

"That was a nice thing to do," said Linda.

"All the players and coaches were wonderful. They were all so happy for us; of course … they had no way of knowing how short-lived that happiness would be. Miguel said he would be looking for me in the stands during the game. I told him I would be sitting about ten rows back behind home plate with several of the wives and girlfriends who were also along for the opening game. I told him I would be looking for him as well."

***

What a day! thought Miguel as he waited for the game to begin. It was the first game of the season, with all the attendant pomp and ceremony. Three different people threw out the "first" pitch. The national anthem was sung by a country singer he didn't recognize. Jets from a nearby Air Force base flew over at the end of the anthem. Yet all Miguel could think about was Isabella. *God, she is so wonderful. I'm going to get to grow old with her.*

He knew he had to get his mind on the game. He had seen Isabella in the crowd and they waved to each other. *Okay, what is this guy going to throw to me? I think I did okay against him last year.* Miguel had not been paying much attention to the pregame scouting report on the Braves' starting pitcher. His head was still in the clouds.

First game, first pitch. He'll probably throw a fastball inside to get a strike on me. I think I'll jump on it and ruin the start of the game for him. Before stepping into the batter's box, he turned once more to see Isabella. He was rewarded with her beautiful smile.

He stepped into the batter's box and dug in. He looked out to the mound. *OK. Let's see what—*

The thought never finished. The roar of the sniper rifle rang out, Miguel collapsed and the whole stadium sat stunned for a moment. Then panic ensued.

As it became clear that Miguel had been shot, fans stampeded for the exits. Over three hundred people were injured in the melee that followed, but fortunately, no one else died. Only one fan headed *toward*, rather than away from, the field: Isabella Cabrera.

As she reached the screen that protects against foul balls, she was greeted with the most horrific sight imaginable: the love of her life, Miguel Fernandez, lying in a pool of blood that was accumulating faster than the ground could absorb it.

Two teammates had rushed to Miguel's side while everyone else on both teams charged through their dugouts and inside to their respective clubhouses. The two friends of Miguel instantly recognized there was nothing they could do for him. He was gone. The echo of the shot had subsided and all they heard now, amid the chaos, were Isabella's screams.

***

"I couldn't get to him," Isabella sobbed. "The police told me that he died instantly, but who knows. Maybe I could have held his head and he might have sensed I was there for him at the end."

Linda had no idea what to say. She had seen death before, but never like this.

"Only two of his friends on the team tried to help," she went on. "The rest just ran and hid. I'll never forget that, or forgive them. When his family was making funeral arrangements, I told them that only those two players should be allowed to help carry Miguel's body to the grave. They honored my request.

"The two, Mario and Miles, I will always remember for their bravery. They shielded Miguel's body from any more bullets and from the cameras, but of course, it was too late for Miguel and too late to prevent the whole world from seeing."

Linda too was in tears. "Isabella, once again, if there is anything I or my agency can do, please ask."

"Linda … I know that it was not those marines. Whoever it was, I'm positive it was under orders of the Cuban government. Please, find the person who did this to Miguel."

"We'll do everything we can, I promise."

27

Tommy had dozed off in his den watching the Braves play the Pirates on the wide-screen TV. The last he remembered, the Braves were leading 3–1. The vibration of his cell phone brought him instantly awake. As he dug the phone from his pocket, he noticed that the Braves had widened their lead to 5–1. *Way to go, Bravos!*

The caller ID showed a number Tommy didn't recognize. Then came a familiar voice. "Hi Tommy, it's Greg Palkot. I'm sorry I'm calling a little late. How are things going back there?" Tommy noticed the word *back* and not *up* or *down,* which would have given some idea of where he was calling from. *Good,* Tommy thought. *I hope they're both being this careful all the time.*

"Hi, Greg," Tommy replied. "There's not much happening here, but we were right about Paul Randolph."

"Meaning …?"

"I talked with Bill Stoner a couple of hours ago—he still has his contacts from before he was suspended," said Tommy. "Randolph has been pressing people at FBI headquarters to let him charge you and Mark for tampering with the investigation into your daughter's kidnapping. The Atkinsons and I believe that he will eventually try to charge both of you in the Kucherov killings—as retaliation for your daughter being taken."

"That's ridiculous!" Palkot exclaimed. "Did he forget that we were in jail?"

"That's a bit sketchy," Tommy explained. "Mark was in custody immediately after Miguel's shooting, but you didn't turn yourself in until a couple days later. Randolph is trying to make the case that you killed the Kucherovs before you gave yourself up."

"That's bullshit!"

"Yes. None of us believe that. I'm just telling you what the asshole is trying to do."

"Is he making any progress?"

"Not so far. I hope that the people at the top of the food chain see what kind of guy he really is. That would be good for us," said Tommy.

"It would be," Palkot agreed, "but I think I'll stay away awhile longer. I'll advise Mark to do the same. Anything else?"

"Linda talked to Isabella again," said Tommy. "The girl has no idea where the Cuban guards might be and has little else to offer. She's only now coming out of her shock. She and Linda have formed a bond and they're starting to talk."

"OK then. Keep us up to speed. One of us will call in a couple of days. With a different phone."

"Talk to you soon."

As he got off the phone, Tommy noticed the Braves' closer was doing his job, and minutes later, the final score was Braves, 5–2.

His conversation with Linda that afternoon brought back memories of the night of the shooting. Tommy and his father were at the stadium for opening night and were just settling in when they heard the loud sound of what turned out to be a rifle. At first, Tommy thought it was a last bit of pregame firework; but fireworks would not have sent Fernandez bleeding to the ground.

All around them, people clamored for the exits. "Let's stay put," Tommy said to his father. "If the shooter was interested in killing more people, there would be a lot more shots."

That decision proved fateful: neither Cevilli was injured, as were so many others in the stampede. That game, and the entire slate of games that followed, was canceled for four days while Major League Baseball tried to get a handle on what happened at SunTrust Park.

A consensus had been reached among baseball executives, that Fernandez had been a solitary target, for reason or reasons unknown. No more shots were fired at SunTrust Park or any other stadium. With stepped-up security around all of the baseball stadiums and the presumed shooter in custody, the season was resumed on the fifth day after the shooting.

At first, attendance had taken a hit, plunging almost 25 percent compared to the previous season; but in the last several weeks, the fans were returning, almost as if nothing ever happened. Staying out of the way of local and federal law enforcement, the office of the Commissioner of Baseball assisted however it could with the criminal investigation. The release of the two marines raised the question, *If they didn't do it, who did?*

Baseball executives hoped the beefed-up security would help to deter any similar future acts, though to allay such a collective fear in the absence of a motive is difficult. None of them knew why Fernandez had been shot.

The YouTube video of Miguel's last at-bat was an internet sensation. Far more graphic than the Zapruder film of

JFK's assassination, the video was viewed more than twenty million times. Several dozen times, it crashed the servers. The public was obsessed with the gory sight..

As much as Tommy enjoyed the memory of Sid Bream's historic slide, he knew that the shooting of Miguel Fernandez would inhabit his baseball dreams for as long as he lived.

28

Paul Randolph stepped from the elevator on the third floor of Atlanta's FBI field office. He was impeccably dressed in a two-thousand-dollar suit and Hermès tie that set him back over two hundred bucks. He complemented the ensemble with Gucci loafers and colorful socks from Unsimply Stitched.

His impeccable style masked his panic. Randolph's plans to put a quick end to the investigation of the shooting of *that fucking Cuban ballplayer,* as he thought of Miguel, were in tatters. The goddamn Cobb County district attorney had set the two marines free; even worse, his own agency was pushing back hard on his plans to re-charge them under federal kidnapping statutes.

The conference room Randolph commandeered was occupied by five field agents actively working the case. In the eyes of the public, their objective was to uncover the conspiracy involved in the Palkot kidnapping and to bring those criminals to justice; yet the men at the table knew that Randolph's goal was to tie that case neatly up with the Fernandez shooting—however he could. He would then ride the wave of public admiration all the way to the directorship of their agency. None of the five at the table that day felt anything but disdain for this jerk.

"All right, gentlemen," Randolph began. "What have you got for me? Surely by now, you geniuses must have something."

Ken Christopher, the most experienced agent—now that Bill Stoner had been suspended—replied. "Sir, we've found out quite a bit more about the Kucherovs, both the older couple and their son."

"Let's hear it," said Randolph.

"First, the son. We've spoken with a number of his friends both from high school and his job. He didn't go to college; he probably couldn't have gotten in with those grades. Records show his IQ was high enough, but he either didn't give a shit or, more likely, had some form of learning disorder."

"My heart bleeds for him," said Randolph, curt. "So for whatever reason, he was a dumb fuck. What's that got to do with anything?"

"It seems," Christopher explained, "that the boy had expensive tastes that couldn't be supported by his jobs as a busboy and convenience store clerk. He got into dealing drugs, strictly small time, and then used what he made from those sales to gamble."

"Would you fucking get to it?! I've got better things to do than listen to some punk's biography."

"Bottom line: there is a group of Russian mafia making heavy inroads into the Carolinas and Georgia. They're out of Florida. They specialize in betting on college football. Their tactic is to let a guy win some easy bets, and then steer him into losses.

"The gamblers have inside sources at many schools. When a college football player is injured, the team is not required to notify the press or anyone else—doing so would significantly change the point spread on some games. The gambling syndicate has access to that information, while the public does not. Pretty soon, young Sergei was racking up some very large losses."

"How do the schools get away with not giving out that information?" asked Randolph.

"Because up until now, all bets on those games were illegal and schools had no obligation to give out information that presumably would make the point spread more accurate. With the new laws allowing sports betting, the colleges will be pressured to give out that info. They won't have much choice, considering who they're up against. The pros have released injury information for years. Colleges have been more fertile ground for the gambling syndicates."

"You mean organized crime," said Randolph. "I'd think that the mob would be happy to have that information kept from the public. The syndicate has ways of getting it and using it to their advantage, while the general public wouldn't.""

"You'd think so, but it doesn't work that way," said Christopher. "The mob has to allow everything to *appear* to be on the up and up, or the legal gambling could be shut down. They figure to eventually own a good part of the legal betting syndicates, just like they do the casinos. The money involved will be huge."

"OK, so …?" asked Randolph.

"So, like I said, young Sergei ran up quite a tab. He went crying to Mom and Dad to bail him out. They took out a second mortgage to cover their kid's debt to prevent the Russians from killing him. The kid promised he was done gambling."

"Like a drunk tells you he'll never have another drink," Randolph scoffed.

"Right," said Christopher. "But no surprise, he ran up another tab. The parents were tapped out. According to neighbors who were friends of the couple, their son told them that if they would help the Russians with some kind of job, the gambling syndicate would cancel his debt. Otherwise, they would kill him. It seems they felt they had no choice."

"So, you're saying that the Kucherovs kidnapped the Palkot kid?"

"No. We don't think they were involved with the actual abduction. The couple just guarded the kid and also her mother, when she came to stay with them."

Randolph looked puzzled. "If all the Kucherovs ended up dead, why did the kid and mom get released?"

"That's a damn good question," said Christopher. "We figure that the Kucherovs sensed it might end badly for the pair, so they freed the mother and daughter as soon as they got word that the 'ransom' had been paid—that ransom being the shooting. Most likely, the kid and the mom would both be dead if the couple hadn't freed them."

"How did they know that the shooting was the ransom demand?"

"We can't find an answer to that. We may never know. Molly Palkot said the couple knew that her husband had done what was asked of him, and they were released."

"So the Kucherovs weren't being watched?" asked Randolph.

"Apparently not. I'm sure the couple were told they were being watched every minute, but they would have been easy to fool. And the life of their son was on the line. In the end, they decided on their own to let the girl and her mother go."

"And then they both got killed. Why didn't they run?" Randolph wondered aloud.

"I think they believed their son was still alive and they would get him back. In fact the kid was dead at least three days before the parents were shot, but they couldn't have known that. When they went to pick him up, that's when they were killed."

"So ... that means Palkot killed them up in Charleston, and then headed back down to Atlanta."

"That doesn't make any sense, Paul. Why would a guy have his daughter kidnapped, then have his ex-wife join the abductors, and then kill the people holding his family? That dog don't hunt."

"Save your fucking redneck colloquialisms for somebody else! I think Palkot wanted his daughter and ex-wife dead because they were costing him money. If they were dead, no alimony or child support. He probably wanted the couple to kill the daughter and ex-wife, and when they didn't, he killed *them*," Randolph concluded.

"But why kill Fernandez? And how would the Kucherovs have known that the 'ransom' had been paid?" Christopher wanted to know.

"That's what Uncle Sam is paying you assholes to find out. Get with it," Randolph ordered them as he rose to leave. "You need to get me something, and I want it fast."

After Randolph departed, Christopher asked the remaining four agents, "Is he really stupid enough …?"

"I don't know," said Jack Kelley, an agent for almost ten years, "but that's where he thinks he's gotta go."

"If he becomes director, he'll ruin the agency," said Christopher. "Let's find out what really happened—and preempt that fucker. Sooner the better. Already, we're running out of time. What say?"

Nobody disagreed.

29

Vinny Funicello and Pete Rosetti were enjoying dinner at The Sicilian Pizza Kitchen in Aventura, on the north end of Miami, less than two miles from Gulfstream Park in Hallandale. This little restaurant, tucked away in a strip mall, had been one of Pete's favorites for years.

"Is that roasted artichoke fuckin' amazing or what?" asked Rosetti.

"I have to admit it's pretty damn good," said Vinny. "I'll never forget the first time I had to eat one of these things. I was at a big party with some of my bosses, and I had no idea how to eat it. I was chewing on the leaves and ignoring the best part-the heart."

"You must have really looked stupid, chewing on those leaves," said Pete.

"Yeah, but I learned pretty quickly. So anyway, why the fuck did you want to meet? We could have just talked on the phone."

"I've been getting the feeling that my phone might be tapped. I keep hearing these strange clicking noises every time I'm on my land line, and also some strange sounds on my cell. I don't know if it's the feds or what."

"Why would anyone be interested in tapping your phones?" Vinny challenged. "That doesn't make sense."

"I don't know what to tell you." Rosetti shrugged. "I just don't want any trouble, for either one of us."

"Okay. So, what's going on?"

Speaking softly, Pete answered. "I just wanted to give you a report on business. The story I put out about you being responsible for Fernandez' death has been great for us. At first, while collections were up, new business was down. But the last week, I've put more money out on the street than any week since I started working for you."

"That's great, Pete." Vinny smiled. "I just might have to put a little extra in your envelope this week."

"That works for me," Pete laughed.

After finishing their meal, Rosetti had a suggestion. "Hey, Vinny. Let's go through the kitchen. I want you to meet Sal, the chef. He's a great guy."

They went back and exchanged pleasantries with Sal. As the chef returned to work, Rosetti said, "Let's just go out the back here. We don't have to go through the whole fucking dining room. It'll be a lot quicker."

The two proceeded down some steps into a deserted area behind the restaurant. "Shit, man," Vinny said. "Now we got to walk all the way around the shopping center. My bad knee won't take it. We should just go back through the restaurant."

Out of the corner of his eye, he saw someone dart from behind the dumpster right beside them, but he was too slow to stop the syringe plunging into the side of his neck. Vinny's last thought was, *that fucking Rosetti.*

A black sedan pulled up, and Rosetti and the man with the syringe threw Vinny into the trunk. The drug would keep him unconscious for two hours, but Vinny had less time than that to live. The driver, careful not to exceed the speed limit, took them to a warehouse Vinny owned in North Miami.

Funicello, unconscious, was removed from the trunk and carried into an area he'd often used as an office to handle his loan-sharking business. The three men, including Rosetti, were greeted by a dark figure inside the office.

"Rosetti, I just need *you* to stay. You other guys beat it. Remember, if I hear a word, anything at all, you won't have happy endings."

"Big Wes" Scarpetta and Mickey "the Mick" Ippolito headed out the side door, pronto.

The man in waiting instructed Rosetti. "Let's get him up. It'll take the two of us to lift him. He's a big motherfucker. What's he weigh, a ton?"

"I think close to four hundred pounds. I hope you ate your Wheaties."

Taking a coil of heavy rope from under a desk, the man tossed it over a steel beam near the ceiling; then he placed the already fashioned noose around Vinny's neck. Using pulleys, they hoisted him until he was the height of the chair off the floor and tied off the rope. Vinny started to regain consciousness. He thrashed and kicked wildly, but to no avail. In less than five minutes he was dead. His eyes bulged from their sockets and his tongue lolled from his gaping mouth. Yet even in death, Vinny's face seemed to be smiling. It was Vinny's last grin.

When the two were sure that Funicello was dead, they arranged the chair to look as if it had been kicked away. A typed suicide note was placed conspicuously on the desk, and the pulleys used to hoist him were discarded.

The SunTrust Park shooter addressed his confederate. "I thought seriously about killing you too, but decided not to. I might need your help in the future. I hope you have a good alibi set up for yourself."

"Good as gold," said Rosetti.

"It had better be," said the shooter. "If this turns out looking like anything other than a suicide, you'll be the first one the cops come after. They have no idea about me."

"It won't be a problem. And I'll be glad to help you. Any way I can."

Pete Rosetti would now head Vinny's old loan shark business. And it hadn't even cost him an icepick.

30

Mike Atkinson was frustrated. He had other important cases, his clients needed him and he needed them. They were not uninteresting cases. They just were not the SunTrust Park shooter case.

The previous evening, over dinner in their Indian Hills home, Linda had excitedly told him of the progress and frustrations she and Tommy were dealing with. Her account of her latest conversation with Isabella was particularly troubling.

"I don't know how much longer I'll be able to stand not being involved in the shooter case," he blurted out.

"Mike ... you agreed that you would finish up these cases to help earn our keep. You're the best investigator of the three of us. You do more in a day than Tommy and I do in a week. I'm sure they won't take much longer, and then you can join us."

"You know that's crap about me being a better investigator; the two of you are more than adept when it comes down to instinct. It's just … this stuff I'm working on … it feels meaningless with a shooter out there."

"When rent and payroll come due, it is *very* meaningful," Linda assured him. "The shooter case isn't bringing that in. Do you think Susie or Amy or even Tommy would want to skip a paycheck because you were no longer interested in the paying jobs?"

"I know that's true, and no, I don't want to miss paying anyone; but Susie thought of something, a terrific idea."

"Susie?"

"Yes. She suggested that we turn some of the easy things over to her. She can do a lot of things under our PI license; and she *is* studying criminology, after all."

"So, what are you proposing?" asked Linda.

"Most of what I've been doing is simple surveillance and interviews. She can do both. She's very good with a camera, and she has the instincts of a Spanish Inquisition interrogator."

"That's high praise … I *think*," said Linda. "But we'll have to pay her more if she's doing actual investigating."

"No, we won't," Mike insisted. "She says she doesn't want more money to do it, she wants the experience. It's worth a try. If I felt the clients would be short-changed in any way, I wouldn't even think about it. But I think she'll do well. And Amy will be here to answer phones or deal with any walk-ins."

"Okay. It's fine with me. I know that you're miserable on the sidelines. What part do you want to handle?"

"I want to follow up on the Kucherov deaths. I can drive over to Charleston and do some digging there. I'd also like to help Tommy chase down those rumors about possible gambling and deals with loan sharks. I'll talk to Gil Torres in Miami about that, and even go down there if I think it might help."

"All right, Mike," Linda agreed. "Do whatever you think will help. We can sit down with Tommy in a couple of days and compare notes. Let's solve this and get back to *paying* gigs."

"Good. I'll call Susie now and get her up to speed. She'll be thrilled. Then tomorrow, South Carolina, early."

***

Mike felt like a new man. The nearly five-hour drive to Charleston had gone by in a flash. He had Sinatra playing the whole way. Since he was alone, he even sang along; Frank was undoubtedly spinning in his grave, *But what the hell,* he thought

237

in his best Frank persona, the crooner's voice playing in his mind. *It feels good.*

Mike loved Charleston. As much as he enjoyed living in the Atlanta metropolitan area with all of its restaurants and sports venues, he'd always felt that to truly sense what being a Southerner is about, you had to go to either Charleston or Savannah.

When visiting those two cities, you see Spanish moss draped from every tree branch and kudzu everywhere you look. No one is ever in a hurry, and the lilt of the accent would bring a smile to anyone possessing even the slightest bit of appreciation for a slower, more genteel pace of life.

Upon arriving, Mike headed for the office of the South Carolina Highway Patrol. He had called ahead and set up an appointment with Captain Spencer Helman, who had headed the Kucherov murder investigation—make that *investigations,* since the murder of the son, Sergei, was a separate matter.

Helman, an affable man in his early forties, had agreed to meet Mike, thanks to a call from their mutual friend, Gil Torres, of the Miami police.

After a few minutes of exchanging pleasantries, Mike got down to it. "I'm sure Gil told you that I'm not working for any law enforcement agency," he began. "We were approached by Greg Palkot and then Mark Alan, the former snipers who were arrested and charged in the shooting."

"Yeah. I'm pretty up to date on the case. I've been following it since it became clear that it was connected to the Kucherov murders."

"Right. The feds think they have it all tied up, nice and neat. Have you met Paul Randolph with the FBI?"

"I sure have," said Helman. He looked dubious.

"I see we feel the same about him," said Mike.

"Hey," Helman suggested, changing the subject. "I know you just got here, but it's almost lunchtime. Hungry?"

"I'm actually starving, but I don't want to waste your time."

"There's a great place down the street where we can eat and talk."

Mike agreed and they headed out.

As they lunched on soft-shell crab po' boys, a Charleston variation of the New Orleans staple, Helman spoke of several possible witnesses he had mentioned to the FBI but whose stories had seemingly been ignored. Paul Randolph had interviewed them.

"The agency had one guy I thought was a pretty decent investigator, Bill Stoner. Funny name for a fed. Anyhow, he wanted to follow up with the people I mentioned, but Randolph shut him down. I guess those witnesses might have screwed up the narrative he was putting together."

"You're right about Stoner. He is a good guy, and he's been suspended by Randolph."

"No shit?" said Helman. "Well, I'm not surprised. Too bad, though. The FBI needs all the good guys it can get."

"I couldn't agree more," said Mike. "So, tell me about those witnesses. I know you can't get messed up with a federal case by stepping on Randolph's toes. But I can do just about anything I want as a private investigator. No jurisdictional barriers."

Helman told Mike about two people he should consider. One was a friend of the murdered son, Sergei. The other was the next-door neighbor of the Kucherovs.

After finishing the lunch and thanking Helman for his help, Mike headed out to see Sergei's friend.

***

Gary Krause worked at a convenience store about fifteen miles from downtown Charleston. He was sandy-haired with a friendly smile. He told Mike that he was about to go on break, and they could talk outside.

"Like I told the other guy, I knew Sergei for three or four years. When we first met, he was working here at this store. He got fired for selling drugs to customers."

"Do you know if he was a user himself?" asked Mike.

"I think he got into the stuff occasionally, but it wasn't like he was messed up all the time. He was selling weed and a little cocaine. He told me that he got it from some Russians he knew."

"I hope *you* never bought from him?"

"No. I wanted no part of that shit. I've been trying to save up enough to get married. My girl, Darlene, would have nothing to do with me if I used drugs."

"Darlene sounds like a keeper," said Mike. "Do *you* have any idea what happened to Sergei?"

"I don't. I saw him about a week and a half before he went missing. He asked me if I had any money I could lend him. When I laughed, he got pissed. He said he was in big trouble and needed ten thousand dollars fast, or he was likely to be killed."

"Did he say who he thought was going to kill him?"

"He didn't use names. He just referred to them as *those goddamn Russians.*"

"Did he say it was the same Russians who supplied him with drugs to sell?"

"He didn't say. He just said he needed to get the money fast."

"Did he tell you why he owed them the money?"

"No. He just said that he'd really fucked up. I know that Sergei had always been a gambler. He used to brag when he won a little, and bitched when he lost. But I thought he was strictly small time; when he asked me to loan him that amount, it was obvious he had gotten in way over his head."

"Do you know where he placed his bets? Did he have a bookie or a regular guy that took his action?"

"He used to spend a lot of time on the phone when he was working here at the store. The boss was always telling him to stop making calls on company time. If he hadn't gotten caught selling drugs, he probably would have gotten fired for just being a shitty employee."

"Did you ever hear him actually placing bets?" asked Mike.

"No. He was very private when making those calls. He usually used the phone in the back room. It was obvious that he didn't want anyone hearing him."

"I get the feeling that you liked him, though."

"Sergei was a good guy. He wasn't the smartest kid in the world, but he didn't deserve to get shot in the face."

"Very few people would deserve that," agreed Mike. "Is there anything else you can tell me about him that might help me figure out who the killer was?"

"When he worked here, he used to talk about a bar where he hung out. I never went there with him and I don't even know where it is. It might have nothing to do with anything. Just a place he'd go to chill and get a drink and maybe shoot a little pool."

"Do you remember the name of the place?"

"I don't remember exactly. I think it's just a man's name, Danny's or Denny's or something. I'm sorry that I'm not more help."

"Gary, I'm glad you were willing to meet with me. You can't tell me more than you know."

"Like I said, I wish I could tell you more. I hope you're able to find out who killed him."

"I hope so too."

***

Well, that was a waste of time, Mike thought. He *already* thought it likely it was Russians. Now, a bar with some man's name—one that the kid didn't even know. This visit so far had yielded nothing.

Twenty minutes later, he arrived at the neighbor of the elder Kucherovs. Yellow crime scene tape still stretched across the home of the murdered couple next door.

After ringing the doorbell, Mike was greeted by a pleasant-looking woman, late fifties or so. After identifying himself and the reason for his visit, he was invited in. The woman introduced herself as Edna Evans. She explained that her husband, Sam, was at work at a local middle-school where he was head of maintenance.

"I will be glad to do anything I can to help catch the people who killed the Kucherovs," she told him. "It about scared Sam and me to death, them living right next door."

"I'm sure it was scary, Mrs. Evans. But the killing wasn't random. I'm quite sure it had something to do with the murder of the baseball player in Atlanta. I don't think you and your husband, or any of your neighbors, for that matter, have anything to be afraid of."

"That's what the local police told us," she said. "And please, call me Edna. Mrs. Evans is my mother-in-law—or rather, was, God bless her soul."

"Okay, Edna. Captain Spencer Helman with the state police thought you might have some information that could help us catch whoever did this. I understand the FBI didn't question you or your husband?"

"Well, one man did ask some questions and I answered best I could, but it seemed like he was hardly paying attention," said Edna.

"I couldn't understand it. On the police shows I watch, they always question the neighbors of the victims. That man with the FBI seemed like he was just not interested in what I had to say. He asked a few questions and then left. The only one we *did* speak with that seemed interested in the answers was Mr. Helman."

Mike nodded silently.

"The man from the FBI, I believe his name was Mr. Randolph, didn't even thank me for talking to him. Oh, I'm being so rude. Could I get you a cup of coffee or something?"

"A cup of coffee sounds great," said Mike, "if it isn't too much trouble." *Randolph...that figures.*

"Oh, it's no trouble," said Edna. "Let's go out to the kitchen and I'll brew us a fresh pot."

When they entered the kitchen, Mike felt he had gone back in time. The kitchen was a virtual replica of his mother's kitchen he had grown up in as a kid back in Atlanta, right down to the Formica countertops, white Frigidaire appliances, and the flour and sugar cannisters next to the stove. There was even a toaster cover in the shape of a nesting hen. He almost expected his mom to walk in.

"I apologize for the state of the kitchen," said Edna. "We've just never got around to updating it. My Sam says I cook just fine here the way it is, and why mess with a good thing?"

"Edna ... I love this room." He looked around. "I bet you even bake your own bread, don't you? And did I just see you put eggshells in with the coffee to brew?"

"Yes, I did. I've been doing that all my life. It's my little coffee secret."

Mike smiled in surprise. "Edna, my mother does exactly the same thing. And that wonderful smell of your bread. I couldn't help but notice the breadbox with the unsliced loaf on top of it."

"You are the observant one," said Edna, impressed. "That must pay off in your business ..."

Mike said, "Edna, if you ever get to Atlanta, I have to introduce you to my mom."

"I think I'd like that," said Edna.

The coffee was ready and Edna poured each of them a cup. They took a seat at the kitchen table and after a bit of small talk, Edna said to Mike, "I believe you want to talk about the Kucherovs."

"Yes," Mike said, rapt. "Anything you can tell me."

"Yes, well. They moved in next door a little over ten years ago. My Sam and Ivan—that was Mr. Kucherov's name—got along great from day one. They loved their yards and were always talking about the best fertilizers and things to make the grass look its best. Believe it or not, one day Olga—that was Mrs. Kucherov's name, of course—well, she and I sat listening to those two go on for over an hour debating on the best length to keep the grass at when they cut it."

"How did you and Mrs. Kucherov get along?"

"That took a little longer. She was shy, though you wouldn't know it if you heard the way she'd rib her husband; but she was shy with other folks, so it took longer for us to become friends. She had Sergei at home and we still had our daughter Sharon, but she was three years older than Sergei. Sharon went on to school at Clemson when Sergei was still in high school. I'm glad that she was older."

"Why is that?" asked Mike.

"Oh, there's no doubt that Sergei had a crush on our Sharon. The fact that she was older gave her a good excuse to avoid his advances, if you could call his sad attempts at conversation *advances*. Sharon was glad to go off to college for

248

many reasons; not having to see that boy was just one small part of it."

"What did you think of Sergei?"

"Nothing but trouble for his parents. He was lazy. He probably never would have amounted to much. His parents were both hard workers. They came from Russia, brought up dirt poor. Sergei thought they should just give him whatever he wanted. When they started putting their foot down, he had to get a job, and he got one at a convenience store. Until then, his only other work was as a busboy at a Mexican restaurant, and he was fired after three days for being lazy and sloppy. I believe he gambled away all his earnings from the store, and then some."

"And then some ...?" Mike prodded.

"I know that his parents had to bail him out of his gambling debts at least two times. He came home one night beaten half to death. Olga told me they had to take out a second mortgage to pay off the people he owed or else. Those people ... the people Sergei owed ... were bad people. They were Russians, and Olga felt—she *knew*—that they had targeted her son in some way."

"Do you know what she meant by that?"

"Olga—well, we were friends by then—told me Sergei used to spend time at a bar called Dimmy's. That was the nickname of the owner, Dimitri something or other. A Russian man. Anyway, she told me that when the owner found out her son spoke Russian, he took an interest in him. *Quite* an interest. Got him into gambling. At first, he won a little, then a little more, but when he started losing, he had no way to cover his debts. That's when they had to mortgage their house, after Sergei came home all beat up."

Dimmy's. That was the place Krause was talking about, not Denny's or Danny's. "Edna, how long ago was that?"

"Just under a year ago. Olga told me that Sergei promised that he would quit gambling ... but of course, he didn't."

"So, it appears that Sergei got back in debt again. Do you know anything about those recent problems?"

"Olga spoke to me in confidence but ... none of that matters now. She said that she and Ivan were just sick about it. It seems that this time, Sergei was in over ten thousand dollars debt to whoever he was placing bets with. Those people were going to kill him, she said, but she and Ivan could only save his life by doing a job for them."

"Did she say what kind of job?" asked Mike.

"No, but she did say that they were going away—for a week or longer—and she asked me to watch over their house for them. That was the last time I saw her."

"You have no idea what the job was or where she was going?"

"I'm sorry, I don't. I don't think even she knew at the time."

"Did you tell all of this to the man from the FBI?"

"I tried to. Like I said, he didn't seem interested in what I might know."

"Maybe the folks at Dimmy's have some information?" Mike suggested.

"You won't find anything there," said Edna. "The place burned to the ground about ten days ago, and no one has any idea of where Dimitri is. From what I heard, there was an insurance payout coming, but no one to claim it."

"Was anyone hurt in the fire?" asked Mike.

"No," said Edna. "There was no one inside when it burned, and no sign of any burnt remains."

Wow ... Whoever is behind all this doesn't believe in leaving any witnesses. "Edna, I appreciate your time and I truly appreciate the hospitality. I can't think of anything else to ask. Can *you* think of anything—anything at all—that might help me find out who killed your neighbors?"

"Mr. Atkinson ... Mike ... I truly can't. I wish I could tell you more."

So do I, Mike thought. "If you think of anything else, please call me." He gave her his card.

"I surely will. And I hope God blesses you and you can solve this mess."

***

On his way back, Mike called Linda. "I think I may have wasted this trip to Charleston."

"So there was nothing?" she asked.

"Nothing more than what we already know, including the fact that the Randolph wasn't trying to find out what actually happened.

"I did meet a real nice guy in the state police that you would like. I also met my mother's twenty-years-younger twin sister."

"Your mother's …?"

"I'll tell you when I get home. Any news?"

"Well, yes. It seems Randolph has re-solved the case."

"Re-solved? What the hell does that mean?" asked Mike.

"Remember those stories about Fernandez and the loan sharks? The head shark was found hanged with a suicide note beside him."

"What did the note say?"

"It said that this fat cat—this loan shark czar, one Vincent Funicello—hanged himself because he couldn't stand the *guilt* he felt over having Miguel Fernandez killed. He hadn't been repaid, you see, and according to this suicide note, Miguel had to be killed, to maintain Vincent's credibility with other borrowers."

"That sounds like total BS to me. Fernandez was about to sign a giant contract. He wouldn't have wanted any scandal."

"Tommy and I both agree that it's nonsense. But it gives Randolph another chance to claim that he has solved everything, and take credit."

"Don't tell me: the suicide note was typed."

"Right-o. Another similarity to the Michaels case! But back then, we were pretty sure who the killer was. Now we haven't a clue."

"Whoever it is has been careful—that includes burning down the bar where Sergei Kucherov did his gambling. And there's no sign of the owner, a Russian named Dimitri who probably was Sergei's bookie. I'm pretty sure his chips were cashed in."

"It was good to get Alan and Palkot out of town. They've been calling in regularly and haven't noticed any sign they're being followed. Now, you just hurry up and get home. It was lonely sleeping all by myself last night ..."

Mike smiled as he ended the call.

31

Isabella Cabrera had not had a single full night's sleep since Miguel's death. As she napped fitfully in midafternoon, she dreamed again of his funeral. Her sobs had filled the air as the priest spoke what he hoped would be comforting words in Spanish. *"Miguel era un buen hombre. Está en un lugar mejor. Está con su Señor"*—Miguel was a good man. He is in a better place. He is with his Lord.

No, he's not in a better place! He should be here with me—we'd only just begun our lives! Isabella almost shouted her thoughts upon hearing what were meant to be words of comfort. *How could God do this to Miguel? How could He allow it to happen?* Isabella knew there were no answers to her questions. Throughout the remainder of the funeral she sat stunned, unable to even acknowledge the words of sympathy from the many friends in attendance.

Miguel's casket was carried to the grave by Miles Phelps and Mario Fabriozo, the two teammates who tried to shelter him at home plate moments after the shooting. They were joined by his agents, Pedro Soto and Tomás Santos. Also joining them was Miguel's friend Ira, the dentist–jeweler who had fashioned the beautiful ring Miguel had given Isabella. The last of the pallbearers was an elderly man Isabella didn't recognize, but who attracted a good deal of attention from the attendees. At the graveside, he approached her. He had tears in his eyes.

Speaking in Spanish, the man said to her gently, "Isabella, I am so sorry for your loss. I only met Miguel once, when he was still a boy. I knew then he was destined for greatness. It is beyond tragedy that his greatness has been cut so short."

"Thank you for your kind words, sir. I'm so sorry, but I don't know your name."

"I'm the one who should be sorry for not introducing myself. My name is Tony Oliva."

***

Isabella's dreams were interrupted by a loud knocking on her front door. When she opened it, she was startled to see Miguel's former bodyguards, Juan Escobar and Carlos Fuentes.

"May we please come in? We need to speak with you," said Fuentes.

Remembering the two men from the morning before Miguel was killed, Isabella welcomed them into her home. These two had warned Miguel of the possibility that the Cubans might try to kill him. She was convinced that was what actually happened.

Dios mio—My God. "We all thought that the two of you were dead."

"We would be, if we had not hidden. We have been staying well out of sight," said Escobar.

"The Cubans don't believe in leaving witnesses behind," Fuentes added. "We are positive that Raul Castro ordered Miguel's murder, no matter what nonsense the FBI has been saying. We think we have a way of proving it—and getting the killer—but we need your help."

Over the next hour, the two men laid out an intricate and dangerous plan. Isabella agreed to help them. She would do anything to bring Miguel's killer to justice.

"We must be very careful," Fuentes warned. "One of the people I believe is behind all of this is an old Cuban general. When I was being told how to cheat Miguel out of his money—

believing it would bring his parents to the States—the general was bragging about having Oswald killed after he had 'done the job' for him. He said they would have killed Ruby as well, but he was caught at the scene. They got word to him in jail that if he said anything, his entire family and anyone he had ever known or loved would die horrible deaths.

"Ruby must have believed them: he died in prison without talking. I don't know if the old man's story is true or not. He liked to brag. He was talking to another man there in Raul's office, and he did not notice me listening. The other man seemed familiar with the story and appeared bored by the general.

"He obviously liked to be the center of attention. He was an arrogant bastard with a camouflage eyepatch. It was a hideous-looking thing, but he thought it was *muy elegante*. I learned that he was called Camojo—Camouflage Eye—behind his back, but no one called him that to his face. He would most likely have killed anyone he thought was mocking him. And I'm sure this same old general was involved in Miguel's murder."

Isabella had no idea who Ruby and Oswald were, so she made no comment; *and Camojo? What the hell?*

After the men left, she Googled the names the guards had mentioned: she found no reference to General Camojo, but what

258

she read about Oswald and Ruby nearly floored her. *What have I gotten myself into?* she wondered. *No matter,* she decided. *We will avenge Miguel.*

32

The FBI news conference began promptly at 10 A.M. when Paul Randolph stepped to the podium with its cluster of microphones and a room full of reporters from all of the major network and cable news stations.

"Good morning. For those of you who don't know me, my name is Paul Randolph. I'm the assistant director of the Federal Bureau of Investigation in charge of organized crime activities. I'm here this morning to announce the closing of the investigation into the shooting death of Miguel Fernandez at SunTrust Park.

"Mr. Fernandez was shot and killed by an unknown individual under orders from one Vincent Funicello of Miami, Florida. Mr. Funicello was the head of a loan-sharking operation in Miami, as well as a participant in a large assortment of other criminal enterprises. Mr. Fernandez had utilized Mr. Funicello's services inasmuch as Fernandez had borrowed a substantial sum of money from Funicello's organization.

"Three days ago, Mr. Funicello was found dead. The cause of death was strangulation by hanging. His death by suicide was accompanied by a note, the contents of which I will now read.

'To my family and friends. I am sorry for what I am about to do. I can't take the guilt anymore. I ordered Miguel Fernandez' murder and paid the man who did it. There is no need to look for that man. I had him killed and dumped in the Everglades, where I'm sure, the alligators made fast work of him.

'Fernandez borrowed money from me and did not pay it back in the manner he promised. It didn't matter to me that he would be getting a new contract and would have been able to pay me later. My credibility is based on people meeting my terms on time.

'I did not anticipate the horrible feelings of guilt that I have had to live with ever since his death. I had never killed anyone before, and I had no idea how it would affect me. Doing this is the only way I can see to take away the pain of my guilt.

'Vincent Funicello'

"It is obvious from his note," said Randolph, "that Funicello was wracked with guilt and killed himself because of it. I will take a few questions."

"Mr. Randolph," said the correspondent from NBC News. "First let me congratulate you and the agency for a job well done. But what about the two former marine snipers who you earlier had implicated in the Fernandez shooting? Are they now cleared of those charges?"

"Thank you for your kind words, Jim. The two former snipers to which you refer, Mark Alan and Greg Palkot, were obviously not involved in the Fernandez shooting. There were some mistakes made on the part of local law enforcement in their arrests. Their activity, however, has been shown by my agency to have been only involved with the attempt to obtain the release of Mr. Palkot's ex-wife and daughter, who had been kidnapped.

"I feel *that* crime overlapped the Fernandez shooting, but was not connected. The possibility of new charges against Alan and Palkot has been left open, since they did not properly notify the FBI of the abduction, and may have obstructed my agency's attempts at solving that crime."

"Mr. Randolph!" shouted the Fox News reporter, "are you satisfied with Mr. Funicello's admission in his note that the actual killer is now deceased, but remains unnamed?"

"Why wouldn't I believe him, Greg?" replied an irritated Randolph. "It was the admission of a dying man. Dying men tell the truth."

"If I might follow up, sir? Why are you so sure that the note was authentic and that the scene was not just staged to look like a suicide?"

"Well, Greg, you're going to have to take my word for it. The FBI forensics people are the best in the world. They would not make that kind of mistake. The integrity and reputation of our agency depends on getting things right. I have every confidence that they got this one right, too."

As a number of other reporters shouted out questions, Randolph addressed the crowd. "Guys, that's going to be all the questions I can take. I have a plane to catch to DC. I have a meeting scheduled with the interim director."

Randolph left, leaving behind a shouting, frustrated mob of newsmen.

***

Six hundred and fifty miles south of the downtown Atlanta press conference, a man sat at a corner table of a popular

Miami sports bar, watching the event on television. At its conclusion, he rose from his barstool.

"Gringo pendejo," he said under his breath, clearly directed at Paul Randolph. Then, with only a hint of a grin, the SunTrust Park shooter left the bar and headed for his car.

33

"I don't fucking believe it," fumed Tommy. He, along with Mike and Linda, as well as Bill Stoner, had watched Randolph's press conference on the TV in Linda's office.

"That was right out of Grimm's Fairy Tales," said Mike. "Does he really think the public is going to buy that crap?"

"Obviously *he* does," said Linda, "but not so much those reporters. He ducked their questions fast enough."

Bill Stoner was irate. "This is exactly what I expected from that jerk. Some of the things he said: *Dying men tell the truth. Agency integrity. Our guys would not make that kind of mistake.* That is such bullshit! I guarantee the FBI forensics people never even got to voice an opinion. Randolph saw a chance to close the case and take credit. That's all there is to it."

"To say nothing about 'local authorities making mistakes'—and that the Palkot kidnapping overlapped but is *'not* connected' to Miguel's shooting. The lies are obvious and suit his narrative," Tommy noted.

"The local police are going to be very upset. The shooting wasn't even a federal case. Randolph used the kidnapping connection to worm his way into the investigation and used anything he thought might further his agenda."

"The question is," asked Tommy, "what are we going to do now?"

"Mike and I have some thoughts on that," said Linda. "Isabella called me last night with some interesting news: yesterday, Miguel's former bodyguards paid her a visit."

"Escobar and Fuentes?" Stoner whistled. "I would have bet anything that they were dead."

"They definitely are *not* dead. And they had a very interesting idea on how to expose the real killer. After Randolph's press conference, Isabella should be even more anxious to implement their plan."

"What do the guards have in mind?" asked Tommy.

After Linda detailed the Escobar–Fuentes plan, she asked for thoughts.

"We need to get Alan and Palkot involved," Mike suggested. "Because of the shooting and the subsequent attempt to frame them, those two almost lost everything. I think they would very much like to be in on this. And their input will be invaluable."

"Great idea," said Linda. "If we expose the real shooter, they'll be able to breathe easier. They seem to be the only people involved with the shooter who haven't been killed yet. I don't know what the full story is, but I'd bet a small fortune that Vinny Funicello had nothing to do with Miguel's shooting."

"Or the Kucherov killings," Mike added. "I'm certain all of these incidents are connected, and Funicello was not the guy.".

Everyone agreed.

34

Isabella Cabrera had always possessed great self-confidence: first as a girl, and now as a woman. Growing up as a second-generation Cuban in Miami's Little Havana district, her parents had raised her right. She was taught that beauty, which she unquestionably possessed, is only skin deep; and that what is inside a person, their heart and soul, is what matters.

She well remembered, as a very young girl, laughing once at another girl's unfortunate looks in the presence of her mother.

Hearing Isabella's cruel mockery, her mother said, "Isabella, do you think that little girl went to a store and picked out her face? No, she didn't. It is the face that God has given her. I'm sure that if she had a choice, she would be pretty like you, but she didn't have that choice.

"But that little girl might be more beautiful on the inside, where people can't see. If she was the pretty one and you weren't, she might not have made fun of you like you did of her.

Just remember that, Isabella. You were laughing at God's work. We get what God gives us on the outside. We can choose what we will be on the inside."

She never forgot that.

Her father had taught her a valuable lesson as well: to be cautious of people interested only in her appearance, especially boys. He confessed his own boyhood follies, that he hadn't always behaved appropriately toward the opposite sex; he had, like many of his friends, treated girls as something to be conquered.

"Isabella ..." she remembered him saying, "you are a very beautiful young woman ... many boys and men will be drawn to you. It gives you amazing power over them, but you must not abuse that power."

He made sure she understood she was not just beautiful on the outside but on the inside as well. "You deserve a man in your life who recognizes that. Someday, you will have that man." Her thoughts drifted to Miguel. Here was a man who always met her eyes. Miguel ...

Ever since meeting him at a South Beach club, Isabella had been enchanted with this man. She had been the only person in the room who did not know that he was the most eligible bachelor in all of Miami, if not the entire country. She knew almost nothing about baseball, but this handsome, unassuming young man won her heart from the beginning, and soon won over her family as well. She could not wait until the day they were married.

Now there would be no wedding. There would be no children or happy life together. Miguel had been taken from her in as cruel a fashion as anyone could imagine.

For weeks, she thought—no, *believed*—that she hated God. How could He have allowed this to happen? Finally, she realized the futility of hatred and concentrated on what God had given her: Miguel. If only for too short a time! But it was a wonderful time, however short. One thing was certain: whoever had done this horrible thing must pay.

As frightened as she was after hearing the plan conceived by Escobar and Fuentes, she was determined to help carry it out. She was confident, and she would play her part.

35

Jeff Shatz, whose sports columns were a semiweekly highlight of the *Miami Herald* sports page, was surprised by Isabella's call.

"Mr. Shatz, we've never met but I was Miguel Fernandez' fiancée. I would like to sit down and talk to you about him and the recent FBI case ruling—that is, if you're interested."

"I would be very much interested," replied Shatz. "I'm sure you're aware that I, as well as many other writers, have attempted to interview you many times, both before and after Miguel's death, and you always refused. What's changed?"

"I'm outraged by the official closing of the case by the FBI. Their conclusion is nonsense, and I'd like to talk about that. Also, it would be good for the public to know what a wonderful man Miguel truly was, and how tragic his loss, not just for me but for everyone."

"If I may ask," inquired Shatz, "why me?"

"Miguel liked you. He said that you were always fair in your columns, even when you had to say something negative."

"I appreciate hearing that. It's always been my goal. When and where would you like to meet?"

Isabella suggested a time and place and Shatz agreed. The meeting was set for the next day.

Three days later, Shatz's column in the *Herald* aroused the interest and curiosity of people throughout the country.

Jeff Shatz Sports Beat

In a far-ranging interview, the fiancée of murdered Miami Marlins star Miguel Fernandez, who everyone not visiting the moon in the last two months knows was murdered during a game between the Marlins and the Atlanta Braves on opening day, had some very interesting things to say.

Isabella Cabrera, a second-generation Cuban, born and raised in Miami, expressed outrage at the recent FBI press conference wherein Fernandez' murder was proclaimed to have been ordered and paid for by Vincent Funicello, a Miami loan shark and organized crime figure.

Miss Cabrera insisted that she has proof that the murder was, in fact, carried out under orders of the Cuban government,

276

and that she knows the identity of the trigger man. She claims to have gotten irrefutable proof from persons who will remain unnamed, but were proven to be credible to this writer.

Miss Cabrera wants the world to realize what a fine man her fiancé was, and that he was killed for defecting from the communist island state of Cuba, and then arranging for his remaining family members to be smuggled out of Cuba to the United States. Fernandez then continued to be an outspoken critic of the Castro regime. She insists the order to kill Miguel came from the very top, and that she has proof that the Castro brothers were to blame.

Miss Cabrera will hold a press conference on the front steps of the Miami City Hall this coming Saturday morning at 10 A.M. At that time, she says that she will name the true assassin and offer proof of the Cuban government's involvement.

She could not be persuaded to give up that information prior to the press conference. She claims all the world will learn at the same time. Yours truly, and I'm sure many others, will be there for her announcement.

Until next time, I'm Jeff Shatz. See you in the papers.

The members of Atkinson Detective read the column at the agency office. Mike, Linda and Tommy were joined by Bill

Stoner, who lately seemed to be there more often than not, as well as Greg Palkot and Mark Alan. The latter two had been notified by Mike to come to Marietta as surreptitiously as possible. They had arrived the night before.

Alan and Palkot had been read into the plan formulated by Juan Escobar and Carlos Fuentes. Everyone had doubts: the plan posed a substantial danger to Isabella, yet she was determined to follow through with the operation.

The contributions required by Alan and Palkot were substantial and critical if there was to be any chance they could pull it off. They would assist the two Cuban bodyguards in drawing out and capturing the killer.

"Is there any other way to do this?" Stoner asked. "It just seems there is far too much risk for Isabella. I know she's determined to do it, but there's got to be a safer way."

Mike appreciated Stoner's input; *I wonder if he might be interested in working for us in the future?* Storing that thought away, he addressed the group. "I talked with Escobar and Fuentes for over two hours yesterday afternoon. I'm thrilled they're still alive. I didn't think their chances were good. When they told me their plan, I thought they were crazy. But after our discussion, I realize it's probably the only way to get this guy. Everyone knows the danger involved."

"Isabella is the one most at risk," said Linda, "and when she first called me with this idea, I tried my damnedest to talk her out of it. I told her that it wasn't worth getting killed for. She strongly disagreed. She said that the killer took away her life when he killed Miguel, and that the only way she will ever have any chance at future happiness is if the killer is caught and made to pay for his crime. I couldn't talk her out of it. I guess, bottom line, that I agree with her."

"OK. If all agree to go forward, then we should get going. Mark and Greg, you need to get to Miami fast. Linda has you booked on a flight this afternoon at two. That gives you less than forty-eight hours to get everything in place. Can you do it?" asked Mike.

"We were up most of the night talking about it. It's going to be dangerous, but we think we can make it work," said Palkot.

"Greg's right," Alan agreed. "This guy was perfectly willing to have us killed or put in prison for life. It seems only fair that we help nail him."

"Okay," said Linda. "The rest of us will be down tomorrow morning, as soon as we wrap up a few things here.

Let's make this work, and let's be sure none of the good guys get hurt."

"If we are going to do this," said Stoner, "I have some ideas to protect Isabella. I'll get right on it. If I work with our two snipers here, I believe we can carry this out with a minimum of risk."

36

The shooter waited motionless in his undetectable perch across the street from City Hall. The spot had been carefully chosen, and he knew it was perfect. He had set up two hours before dawn and felt certain that he had been undetected.

The Cabrera girl had only to make her appearance and it would all be over. No worries about exposure for himself or his employers. He never expected that anyone would learn his identity, but seemingly the Cabrera girl had, probably from those two fucking Cuban guards that he had been unable to find. The general said that she had to be eliminated.

He had been sure that with the staged suicide of Vincent Funicello, his worries were over. The FBI idiots were sold; why would anyone believe that it had *not* been Funicello?

He couldn't help smiling to himself at the thought of the loan shark's stupidity. Taking credit for a murder he had not committed? Pete Rosetti told him that it had been *his* idea. He related this fact to the shooter as an indicator of his own tactical brilliance, but the man poised with the sniper rifle doubted that 'brilliance' belonged anywhere on Pete Rosetti's resume.

The door opened and a woman he immediately recognized as Isabella emerged along with three other persons. None of the others mattered-only Isabella. She was going to use this highly public venue to name him.

As he focused on his sights and prepared to fire, he detected a slight noise behind him. His concentration never wavered. He took the easy shot which would rid him of this risk.

The shooter barely had time to register that somehow his shot had not found its mark when he felt a crushing pressure on his windpipe. He was held immobile as the force from behind painfully squeezed the life out of him. He vaguely registered the shrill sound that escaped from his own mouth before everything went dark for the last time.

***

After the dust settled, no one among the throng of reporters and others present had any idea what just happened. Everyone had seen an obviously nervous Isabella Cabrera, dressed all in black, approach the collection of microphones that awaited her in front of the Miami City Hall. She was accompanied by a woman whom the reporters were able to discover was Linda Atkinson of the Marietta, Georgia–based Atkinson Detective Agency, who also happened to be a friend of Isabella's. The women were accompanied by two men.

A stage and podium had been assembled the previous day. The construction, with its accompanying safety features, had taken well into the evening to be completed.

No one, outside a handful of security people, were aware of the precautions built around that stage. Large, bulletproof, but virtually invisible panels of reinforced mylar stood above and to both sides of the spot from where Isabella was to speak.

As she approached the stage from under cover of the entry way of City Hall, Isabella was garbed in ultrathin but highly effective Kevlar, which covered her entire torso under her black dress. Linda was similarly protected.

Only moments after Isabella began to speak, the sound of a gunshot rang out and echoed off the buildings, making it hard to tell where the shot had come from. Most believed it had originated from the parking structure directly across the street.

On hearing the shot, the two men who were on the podium—later identified as Mike Atkinson and Tommy Cevilli, of the same Marietta detective agency—pushed Isabella and Linda to the ground and covered them with their bodies.

Both women were unharmed, save for a few scrapes and bruises caused by being shoved to the dais floor. The sniper's bullet had been deflected from its target and, thanks to the protective panels, lost ninety-nine percent of its velocity.

The panels performed perfectly. Not only were they invisible from the shooter's position, but they deflected what surely would have been a fatal shot directed at Isabella. Bill Stoner had come through in acquiring them. They were the same material used to protect the president and other dignitaries in public.

Mike and Tommy continued to shield the women for more than five minutes. When they were quite certain that the danger was over, all got up. Both women were glad to get out from under the weight but even happier to be alive and grateful for their protection. They rushed inside City Hall.

Twenty minutes after gunfire had broken up the press conference, a male was found lying on the fifth floor of the parking structure across the street. Hidden by a small construction area surrounding the opening of the deck to the outside, he was invisible to cars inside the garage. He was also quite dead.

The man had been nearly decapitated by a piano wire garrote left gruesomely in place. His rifle was at his feet along with one expended cartridge. His eyes bulged grotesquely from their sockets. The SunTrust Park shooter would never harm anyone again.

***

"What in the name of God just happened?!" Mike shouted at Tommy, Bill and Linda. "Escobar and Fuentes said they would never let the guy get off a shot! If Bill hadn't gotten us those panels, Isabella would be dead. Maybe Linda too."

The scene of the press conference had been carefully staged by Mike, Tommy, Bill Stoner, and Gil Torres of the Miami Police Department.

Torres was less than honest with his superiors when arranging security for the event, minimizing the danger and requesting a few extra men "just in case." He made no mention that Isabella was to be used as bait, nor would he ever concede that was indeed what just occurred.

The most important part of the staging was the result of Palkot and Alan's expertise. Both were highly trained and knew precisely where a shooter would set up. The marksmen ensured that the position of the podium could be threatened only from the front. Any shooter would have to use the five-story parking deck across the street, from either the fourth or fifth floor.

They knew too he would not be on the roof, as helicopters and observers from other buildings would spot him before he could get off a shot. Below the fourth floor would give him no vantage point.

"Fuentes texted me about thirty minutes after it happened," said Tommy. "He was on the fifth floor with Escobar on the fourth. He claims he slipped while coming up on the shooter and the guy squeezed off a shot."

"It's a damn good thing we had those panels," said Mike. He knew that Isabella's Kevlar would have been unlikely to protect her, given the shooter's propensity for head shots.

Bill Stoner had rushed to the parking structure immediately after the gunshot but was now with the others inside

City Hall. He and Gil Torres had discovered the corpse. No one else was allowed anywhere near the scene.

"We would have aborted if we thought there was any chance of Isabella being harmed," Bill reported to Tommy and the Atkinsons. "We obviously didn't want the son of a bitch to get a shot off but felt certain that the panels would protect her if he did. And they worked perfectly. It was worth all the work in the middle of the night to get them installed."

Stoner and a crew spent over three hours arranging and suspending the protective panels the night before the press conference. Following the direction of Palkot and Alan, Stoner had the panels suspended in place soon after midnight. Both marines felt sure that the shooter would set up shortly before dawn, but not much earlier; otherwise, he would be in too much danger of detection.

Gil Torres had managed to keep the panel assembly out of sight of other Miami police officials.

"There's no way the boys upstairs would have allowed this to happen," Torres said. "I'm going to claim that the FBI arranged it. Even though Bill Stoner is suspended, the agency will still be quick to accept credit. God only knows what might have happened if this had all gone south."

"Thank God it didn't," said Linda, "but a garrote? Fuentes couldn't just shoot the guy?"

"No. No way would they take a chance on being heard. If Escobar or Fuentes could have gotten the drop on the shooter, they would have taken him alive. They insisted on acting alone in carrying out the actual takedown: no law enforcement, local or federal. They felt the shooter was too smart and would spot a setup. Plus, the two guards had to make a getaway. More gunshots would have made that impossible, even silenced ones."

"Had they been able to take him alive," asked Linda, "what would they have done?"

"I believe they would have knocked him out and tied him up securely and called us," Mike said. "Then we would have to explain our finding him. In fact, we would have to do a lot of explaining. Things worked out better this way." He did not voice his belief that survival of the shooter was likely never an option for the Cuban guards.

"Did we *order* a hit on the guy? Are we in trouble?" Linda asked, worried.

"No," Mike assured her. "We played no official part in this. We were here to offer moral support for Isabella. The operation belonged to the Cuban guards. It was very important to them that they not be identified. Their lives wouldn't have been worth a nickel had they been named. They were only willing to speak with the reporter, Jeff Shatz, off the record to establish their *bona fides*."

Linda sighed in relief.

"They want to go back to Cuba, eventually. If it were known that they were responsible for killing this guy, the Cuban government would hunt them down. So, to your question, Linda, we can all sleep easy tonight and still look ourselves in the mirror in the morning."

"Where are Escobar and Fuentes now?" asked Linda.

"Palkot and Alan got them to a small airstrip just south of the city," Mike explained. "By now, they should be on their way to Costa Rica. They'll stay there awhile before heading back to Cuba. There will be 'proof' that they had been there for more than two weeks; we have Stoner and his CIA contacts to thank for that."

"Won't the Cuban government know that this is not a police killing? I mean, a *garrote*? It's like some damn *Godfather* movie." Linda frowned.

"Bill Stoner assures me that as far as the public will know, the shooter got away. He and Gil Torres did a fantastic job of getting the body out of there unseen. That's the way it's going to stay. It will be reported that a rifle was found with no fingerprints, and one expended shell found near the weapon, again, with no prints," said Mike. "Bill and Torres managed to keep the press away."

"Is anyone going to believe this whole story?" asked Tommy.

"Let's hope so," said Mike. "Using Isabella as bait without notifying the Miami police was a risk. If Stoner hadn't convinced me that the combination of his panels plus the staging Palkot and Alan arranged was virtually foolproof, I would have stopped it. They were all positive that it would work and Isabella wanted to go ahead, no matter what."

"The FBI will be happy to accept credit for arranging the protection," Tommy explained, "and will blame Miami PD for allowing the shooter to, supposedly, get away."

"What if something had gone wrong?" asked Linda.

"There would have been no one officially to blame. The operation was strictly off the books—and the Miami police are more than happy to leave it that way. The FBI will claim they were doing a service to protect someone peripherally involved in the Fernandez shooting. They'll find a way to spin it without jeopardizing their Funicello fairy tale," said Mike.

"What about the body?" asked Tommy.

"Gil Torres told me not to worry about it," said Stoner. "I'm sure he's fish food by now. Torres knows that if the Cubans find out we've killed the shooter after we were in contact with Fuentes and Escobar, those guards' lives are as good as over, including the lives of their families. If the shooter's merely missing, and the authorities here appear to be actively looking for him, the Cubans will think he's just gone to ground."

Stoner continued. "We'll make sure the Cubans know we suspect their government and that we will be looking for the shooter, whoever he is, to try to get back to their island. Hopefully, that will give Fuentes and Escobar a chance to get their families out. It seems to be getting easier for people to leave. They'll have the option of returning eventually, when the political climate is different."

Just then, Tommy's phone vibrated and he scanned the message, chuckling. "Fuentes is a funny guy ... he told Palkot and Alan that the piano wire he used on the killer was a string from middle C."

"So?" asked Mike.

"Fuentes claims he has perfect pitch ... he says the last sound out of the killer's mouth sounded just like a middle C."

37

The group gathered two nights later at The Forge, a Miami dining establishment famous for its cuisine and atmosphere: Mike, Linda, Tommy, Bill Stoner, Isabella, her parents, and Miguel's family, which included his parents and grandfather. They decided to meet here rather than a Cuban restaurant, hoping to be less conspicuous. It was the first time that Linda, Mike and Tommy had met the two Cuban families. Bill Stoner had gotten to know them earlier in the investigation.

Mike signaled for their attention. "It's a great relief to finally have this unfortunate affair behind us," he began. "Isabella, your family, Miguel's family—I want all of you to know how sorry we are about Miguel. While his loss is irrevocable, I hope that having the man who shot him gone will help you, in some measure, put to rest this terrible chapter and regain some semblance of your life, which is surely what Miguel would have wanted ...

"It's important that none of us ever reveal the truth of what happened," he continued after a respectful pause. "As far as the public is concerned, *the shooter escaped.* We must be very careful to not have anyone believe differently. The lives of the Cuban bodyguards and their families depend on it." All murmured their assent. They had been told the cover story about the shooter getting away.

"Do we know who the man was, and are we positive that he was the man who shot Miguel?" asked Isabella.

"Yes, we are sure that he was the killer," said Mike. "The video footage from the hall camera at the Omni Hotel didn't reveal much, and facial recognition software had no match for him in any database; but the footage did show a distinguishing birthmark on the shooter's forehead. The man in the parking deck had that same mark. Carlos Fuentes recognized him from a meeting in Raul Castro's office. Coupled with the man's height and build that we were able to see on tape, there is no doubt that he was the shooter."

"Do we know his name?" asked Miguel's father.

"We don't," said Mike, "and likely we never will. But his dental work is distinctly Cuban. Not my field of expertise, but Bill Stoner here assures me that is definitely the case."

"So," Miguel's father asked bluntly, "this entire tragedy occurred because Miguel defected and then raised his voice when that bastard Fidel died?"

"Yes," answered Linda. "That, plus the fact that he was able to get the three of you out of Cuba. There doesn't seem to be any other reason. I'm not sure why the Cuban government thought it necessary to attempt to frame a U.S. Marine sniper for the shooting. The shooter could have just as easily shot Miguel and escaped."

"It would have seemed likely to many people that the Cubans were behind it if it had happened that way," said Tommy. "But if they were able to frame someone else—a former marine sniper, for example—there'd be no international incident."

"That conclusion is spot on," said Mike. "You *are* turning out to be the brains of the organization." He saw the hint of a blush on Tommy's face.

"In fact, *no* blame is being placed on the Cubans," Linda pointed out. "It was all Vincent Funicello's doing."

"I considered that possibility once," said Mike. "Pete Rosetti told me about the insurance policy Miguel purchased to pay his debt if something ever happened to him. I thought Funicello might have been willing to accept the insurance policy proceeds and been content with that. He would have shown all his customers just how tough he was. Then I ruled that out."

"What made you discount it?" asked Linda.

"Two things. First, Vinny was a huge baseball fan and genuinely admired and liked Miguel. I think he planned on extorting more money from him, but he wouldn't have killed him."

"And second?"

"From everything I learned about Funicello, he just wasn't that clever. You could find smarter grapefruits. And there was actually a third reason."

"Which was …?"

"Funicello's suicide note said that the real killer was already alligator food. If so, then who took the shot at Isabella? Dead men don't fear exposure, or fire sniper rifles."

"But to think that the Kucherovs were also killed to make this happen ..." Tommy stared at the wall. "That's just as sad as Miguel's death; it's senseless."

"Especially since no one truly believed that Alan or Palkot was the shooter," said Linda. "What a waste. The whole kidnapping scenario was unnecessary. Those poor Kucherovs!"

"True," said Mike. "From what I've been able to piece together, and with an added bit of speculation, this is how I see it happening. The shooter worked either for, or maybe with, the Russian gambling ring in South Carolina, as well as for the Cuban government. He was an independent contractor.

"He had been hired to kill Sergei Kucherov for not paying his gambling debts. He had also been separately hired to kill Miguel by the Cubans. I believe *he* then came up with the idea to use the kid's parents in a kidnapping plan that allowed him to implicate Palkot as Miguel's shooter.

Somehow he had seen or heard about Palkot's TV interview about being a sniper. That bit of knowledge came in handy. The Cubans would certainly have agreed to this minor change of plans. It would keep both the shooter and the Cubans under the radar."

"I almost forgot about that interview. Learning about that and using it was a master stroke for the shooter," said Linda.

"It was," Mike agreed. "Somehow, though, he was convinced—or his bosses in the Cuban government were convinced—that Isabella really had discovered his identity. He must have figured that she had gotten it from the guards, Fuentes and Escobar. That's why he shot so quickly as soon as she got on the podium. He was afraid that she would blurt out his name first thing. He'll never know that we didn't know who he was; still don't, in fact."

"There's no chance that anyone will try to implicate Mark or Greg in the attempt on Isabella, is there?" asked Tommy.

"No," said Bill Stoner. "They were inside City Hall when the shot was fired. There's plenty of surveillance footage and witnesses to prove that."

"Good. It seems that everyone the shooter came in contact with ended up dead except our two marines and Isabella," Tommy noted. "Thank God he wasn't a hundred percent successful.

"Don't forget that it was likely the intention of the killer to also eliminate Leah and Molly Palkot. We will likely never understand how they were spared."

"I wouldn't doubt if there were other killings he was involved in that no one knows about," said Mike. "In fact, I can't imagine that *not* being the case."

"Espero que ese puta frie en el infierno, con Fidel!"—I hope the bastard fries in hell with Fidel!—Miguel's grandfather cried. No one disagreed.

As the two Cuban families chatted, Mike commented quietly to Linda, "It's going to be interesting to see how this affects our business. Even though we can't take credit for solving the murders, we did accomplish our main twin objectives of getting Alan and then Palkot proven innocent."

"I expect we'll get good publicity," said Linda. "We probably shouldn't discuss it over dinner, but if indeed we get busier, we are going to need more help." She looked at Bill Stoner. "Is that something you might be interested in? I have a feeling there's not much future for you at the FBI."

Mike seconded that. "What do you think, Bill?"

"I believe that we could work something out. You guys have been a breath of fresh air compared to working for Paul Randolph."

"What's going on with him and the bureau? Heard anything?" asked Tommy.

"I've heard good news and bad. The bad is that he didn't get fired. Good news is, he's been demoted. I don't know exactly where he's going; he might end up as the Special Agent in Charge in Fargo, North Dakota."

"Those poor people of North Dakota," muttered Linda. They all laughed.

"Sadly enough, if he had really worked at investigating the crimes rather than providing himself a self-promoting narrative, he might actually have solved everything," Stoner said.

"Since Randolph won't be in charge," Mike continued, "are you sure you don't want to go back to the FBI?"

"My wife and I talked it over," said Stoner. "We agreed that if a local opportunity came along, we'd take it. We love the Atlanta area. It'll take decades for all of the corrupt officials to wash out of the bureau. In the meantime, who knows how many new guys just like Randolph might end up getting hired? No, I'm ready to move on."

"Well then," said Linda, "we definitely need to talk."

"By the way," said Mike, "I got a bit of news from Stan Reznick, who received a call from the baseball commissioner, asking about our firm. It seems they are looking for a group like ours to make recommendations for security around all of baseball, and then oversee it."

"Why would they call Stan?" asked Linda.

"The commissioner and Stan were law school classmates and stayed close," Mike explained. "Stan told the commissioner he was pretty sure we'd be interested, and he wants to schedule a meeting. The commissioner will be there."

"I wonder if the commissioner knows about Stan's parking rates? After three meetings," Tommy joked, "they'll have to raise the ticket prices at all major league games." Everybody laughed.

"It's not that funny," said Mike. "Remember, Stan won't validate any more of our tickets."

"If he lands us the baseball gig, we'll just have to pop for parking." Linda raised a glass. Everyone did their best to enjoy the rest of the evening. The food and wine flowed.

***

They were seated in a private area, entirely unaware of the listening device hidden in the floral arrangement at their table. In a side street adjacent to the restaurant, a retired Cuban general sat in his car, overhearing every word.

"I'm sorry my friend," he said to the shooter, who, of course, was not there to hear him. "I believed that bitch really knew your name and could connect you to me, and then to Raul. I could not let that happen.

"I had to order you to silence her. It appears she had no idea who you were. I should have seen this little ruse coming. I'll have to decide what to do about those bodyguards. Perhaps I will say nothing and force them to help me with another project someday. I suppose it is worth keeping them alive."

Veremos si son tan buenos para mantener un secreto como nosotros—We'll see if these detectives are as good at keeping a secret as we were—thought the general. He sincerely hoped they would be.

Kennedy, Oswald and Ruby were long gone, and those secrets would never come out. Eventually, Miguel Fernandez would be forgotten. He prepared to drive off, taking a moment to adjust his camouflage eyepatch. *We'll see indeed.*

Epilogue

Mike, Linda and the elderly couple entered Mike's mother's condo in Buckhead.

"Mom," said Mike, "I'd like you to meet some new friends of mine, Edna and Sam Evans. They're in town from Charleston."

"It's a pleasure," said Helen Atkinson. "Do come in. I've heard so much about you. Can I offer you a cup of coffee?"

"My Sam and I would love a cup of coffee. Your son tells me that you make yours just like I do."

"You use eggshells?" Helen asked.

"Indeed, I do," said Edna. Both women beamed with smiles. They chatted amicably for several minutes while Mike and Linda sat with Sam.

"Linda, what was it Bogart said in *Casablanca?* 'Louis, I think this is the beginning of a beautiful friendship.' Well, I feel just like Bogey," said Mike's mother.

The two ladies headed to the kitchen, their coffee, and their eggshells.

At almost the very same moment outside of Havana, General Guillermo Gonzalez sat contentedly in the garden in the backyard of his country estate. He puffed lightly on his Montecristo *80 Aniversario* cigar. At just under fourteen hundred American dollars for a box of twenty, they were one of the few luxuries the old soldier permitted himself.

As the general rose to head inside, the thought occurred to him that life had been good, despite his injury defending his country at the Bay of Pigs. The smile, about to spread across his face, was shattered as the bullet entered his head just above the bridge of his nose. A large portion of the back of his skull was blown off as the bullet exited. His camouflage eyepatch remained intact.

On the hillside just under a half mile away, hidden by the lush tropical landscape, Juan Escobar and Carlos Fuentes quietly celebrated. As they gathered their equipment and prepared to leave, Juan said to Carlos, "I guess our time with Palkot and Alan was well spent."

Escobar and Fuentes had spent several weeks in Costa Rica with the two former marine snipers prior to returning to Cuba. Fuentes had recognized the SunTrust Park shooter as one of the men he had seen with Raul Castro in that office two years earlier; that birthmark on his forehead was unmistakable. They had also discovered the identity of the old soldier with the eyepatch.

Three men were present the day Carlos Fuentes was taken from prison and brought to Raul Castro's office: Raul himself, of course, as well as the man now known as the SunTrust Park shooter; the third man present was the one-eyed general, the man known as General Camojo.

These three had set this whole series of murderous events in motion. The shooter and the general were now dead—no doubt spending time in hell with Fidel. Word had it that Raul was not well. He would most likely die a natural death, but then again …

"Do you think Alan and Palkot knew what we planned?" asked Juan.

"I can't speak for them, but I don't think they would be too upset with us," replied Carlos. "After all, we did hit the general in the T-Zone."

Author's Note and Acknowledgments

Fiction may draw on historical figures and incidents to further a story; the Castro brothers and the Bay of Pigs invasion, the kidnapping of Frank Sinatra, Jr., and other examples herein are based on actual events, and all are used fictitiously.

To my knowledge, no one would be able to successfully access the roof of the Omni Hotel in the Battery with a sniper rifle. I would encourage anyone visiting the Atlanta area to take advantage of that city's fine establishments, especially those with fabulous views overlooking SunTrust Park.

My stories about Tony Oliva I owe to my friend Donna, who truly was that young girl who helped Tony learn English. Other bits involving him are presented as accurately as possible, and I hope Tony would be pleased.

I have referred to great advances in the battle against multiple sclerosis in this story, as well as in my previous novel. I truly wish this was a reality. Progress is being made, but the improvements in Ann Cevilli's life have not yet been matched in the real world. Hopefully, that will soon change.

One of the nice things about fiction is that when you need a character, he can magically appear however you desire. It helps if he exists in real life. Ira, my friend of almost fifty years, fits that description. He *is* the person described here.

Actual restaurants and other establishments depicted herein have been drawn as accurately as possible, and I hope they too would be pleased.

My paternal grandmother, Mary "May" Groff Hansmann, always put eggshells in her coffee as she brewed it; she also could feed you a bologna sandwich on white bread with nothing else, and it would be fabulous. Some people, like my grandmother, as well as Edna Evans and Helen Atkinson, just have a magic way about them when they enter the kitchen.

I have been a die-hard Braves fan since my childhood when they were located in Milwaukee, and continuing on when they moved to Atlanta. I attended my first Braves game at age nine and have been cheering for the Bravos ever since. Tommy's description of the night Sid slid, as well as his father's encounter with the young Pete Rose, were events that occurred in my life.

I have no knowledge that mylar panels are used for protection of the president or for anything else; they just seemed like a good idea.

I would like to thank my wife, Deborah Hansmann, and many friends who encouraged me to continue the story of the

Atkinson Detective Agency, born in my earlier book, *Once Bitten*. Who knows, they might be back.

Finally, I would like to thank my editor, Michael Wilde, who has shaped this story into a more compact and, hopefully compelling narrative.

Palm Harbor, Florida, October 2018

54245178R00186

Made in the USA
Columbia, SC
30 March 2019